GUNS ALONG
THE BRAZOS

GUNS ALONG THE BRAZOS

•

Owen G. Irons

AVALON BOOKS
NEW YORK

Iro

Published by Thomas Bouregy & Co., Inc.
160 Madison Avenue, New York, NY 10016

Library of Congress Cataloging-in-Publication Data

Irons, Owen G.
  Guns along the Brazos / Owen G. Irons.
      p.   cm.
  ISBN 978-0-8034-9860-0 (acid-free paper)
  I. Title.

PS3559.R6G86   2007
813'.54—dc22

                                    2007016638

PRINTED IN THE UNITED STATES OF AMERICA
ON ACID-FREE PAPER
BY HADDON CRAFTSMEN, BLOOMSBURG, PENNSYLVANIA

Chapter One

I headed for the house on the run at the first shot. It had come from the house, I was sure of that, and Pa was alone up there with those two men who had ridden in the night before. Pa fed them and let them sleep in the barn. Me, I didn't trust them. That redheaded one, Bouchonnet, he said his name was, had shifty eyes and a cruel mouth I didn't like, and the big young one seemed to be smirking at some secret joke all the time. Mike, he said his name was.

The second shot rang out on the heels of the first and I ran on even faster. I was still holding the axe I'd been using to chop kindling at the woodpile, and I tossed it down. I leaped an old fallen oak we hadn't gotten around to clearing from the yard and raced on.

Then I saw them backing from the house. The red-

1

headed one had his gun at his waist, barrel leveled toward the inside of the house, and I cut quick toward the open barn door, my heart hammering wildly as I scuttled into the corner shadows. I felt like a pure coward, but what was I to do? I didn't have a gun with me, and I couldn't go up against two armed men. I stayed there, shaking like a trapped rabbit, the ripe smells of moldering hay and horse all around me, a shaft of light cutting across the floor through the high greasy window of the barn. The two men stood half a dozen yards away from me and talked. I listened.

"Where's the kid?" Mike asked. I could hear his saddle leather creak as he swung aboard his horse.

"Who knows? It don't matter," Bouchonnet answered.

"He could identify us."

"To who?" Bouchonnet laughed harshly. "Way out here? There's no law for a hundred miles. Besides, nobody's going to trail us to Natchez. A river doesn't take tracks, Twilly."

Then I heard the sounds of their horses' hoofs clopping slowly away. For a long time I crouched hidden in the corner of the barn, afraid they might've changed their minds and were waiting out there to kill me. There was nothing to break the silence but the buzzing of some bluebottle flies and the cawing of a crow far away. I couldn't stay there anymore.

I got to my feet, ashamed that my legs were shaky. I went to the barn door and peered out into the harsh light. Domino, my black and white horse, nickered at me from the back of the barn, wondering when I was going to feed him and take him for his daily exercise.

"Later, Domino," I said without looking back.

Then I started toward the house across the yellow grass yard, afraid to enter it, afraid not to know.

I guess I did already know what I would find, but there was something unreal about the scene. I expected wild anger, but I just went cold, icy cold, My tongue was stuck to the roof of my dry mouth. My heart was a slowly pounding trip hammer.

Pa was curled up on the rough plank floor of the cabin beside the tipped-over table. I sat down beside him. A dark stain spread across the gray wood all around him. I lifted his callused hand and just held it, looking out the door, past the cornfield at the big cottonwood grove beyond.

I couldn't tell you how long I sat there, but the shadows had changed and shortened when I finally rose to do what had to be done. Pa's pockets were inside out and the mattress was thrown from his bed. So they had found our seed money, what little there was of it. His watch was gone too. The gold one that my mother had given him, the one that had her picture inside of it.

That was it. That was the little they had killed my father over.

I had a time of it getting him out to the cottonwood grove where I meant to bury him, for my Pa had been a big man in life. Rough hands, soft eyes, not smiling much after my mother had gone away from us, but good to me and thoughtful. Now he was a slight hump in the dark, loamy earth by the creek.

The shadows cast by the cottonwood trees shifted and fluttered in the breeze and the bright creek slipped past silently. I held my hat in my hand, not having any idea of what to say. I had never been to a real funeral. In this far section of Kentucky there were few people, although I knew someone had been building a place a few miles off, over the ridge. We could see their smoke in the evenings. That had been enough to make my Pa wish to move on.

Well, now he had.

I walked slowly back to the house. I went in and pried up the floorboard near the washstand and pulled out the little chamois sack hidden there. It was our 'running' money, as Pa called it. I looked inside the sack. Forty dollars in ten-dollar gold pieces and two silver dollars. I stuffed the money into my trouser pocket.

Outside again, I crossed to the chicken coops. I let them free in a fluttering squawking commotion. They wouldn't have much chance with the hawks and weasels but I couldn't help that. The milk cow I shooed out of the corral. The rabbits I set free of their pen. They were cottontails we caught from time to time when we found a young one, so they would be all right in the wild.

Then I went back to the barn, got my old saddle from the box and my bridle from the wall peg and saddled old Domino.

"I hope you're up to a long run this morning," I told the paint horse. He watched me warily, maybe sensing something in my mood.

I led Domino out and stood looking at the house. It wasn't big, but it was strong like the man who had built it. A good home, a sturdy sheltering place for these last three years. Now it was nothing but a pile of logs. Because of two killers. Bouchonnet and Mike Twilly.

I would never forget those names or their faces. Because I was going to find them and make them pay for this day no matter how long it took.

I went into the house only once more, to take Pa's Winchester rifle from the wall rack above the stone fireplace and to open his dresser and take out the black gunbelt with the walnut-handled Colt .44 in it. I strapped it on, making a new hole for the belt buckle, Pa's belt being too big for me. Then I snatched up a blanket and rolled it and went back to Domino and swung into the saddle, riding out westward toward the Mississippi River beyond the deep forest.

Natchez, I had heard Bouchonnet say. That was where they were bound, and by riverboat. Very well, I would go the same way.

I did not glance back at the house, not even once. But I could hardly see the trail Domino picked for us for the tears in my eyes.

The boat landing was half a mile upriver near the little town called Gorse. It had hopes of becoming a river city like St. Jo or Natchez, but there was little reason for the big sternwheelers to stop there, really. The area had been trapped out long ago; there were no Indian goods anymore. All the Indians—Shawnee mostly—had moved across the river years before.

Still, the riverboats sometimes stopped at Gorse. When someone wanted a ride down to New Orleans or Natchez, then the man at the landing would run a red flag up the pole to signal the pilot of the riverboat. Sometimes the riverboat men would just ignore the flag, figuring it wasn't worth the time and trouble to pick up two or three people.

I rode Domino up the muddy street of Gorse, a rotting little town built on a mudflat with a small, moody population, none of whom seemed to be doing anything in particular at all. Just north of the town was the landing; long, low and crooked, stretching out into the wide muddy Mississippi. I rode up to the small river freight office.

I tramped up onto the platform. There was a low bench against the wall of the building on the south side. An old man sat, head sagging, asleep. The man at the ticket window wore a round blue cap with a shiny bill. He had spectacles shoved up onto his forehead.

" 'Mornin'," I said.

"What do you want, kid?" he asked unhappily.

"I want to travel down Natchez way on the first boat."

"Do you now?" His spectacles snapped down by

themselves and he eyed me through them suspiciously. "Well, it'll be a while. Maybe an hour, maybe four. The *Mississippi Princess* just left, no more'n an hour ago."

My heart leaped a little. That meant that Bouchonnet and Twilly had probably already started down the river. Well ahead of me.

"Did two men get on board the *Princess*? One of them was redheaded and big, the other—"

"I only come on duty fifteen minutes ago," the ticket agent interrupted sourly. "And I got a lot of work to catch up on. Did you want passage to Natchez or not?"

"Yes, please. Me and my horse."

His manner changed a little when I put a ten-dollar gold piece on his counter. Maybe he'd thought I was just a kid wasting his valuable time, not a paying customer.

Anyway, he gave me a blue ticket about the size of a playing card and a yellow bill of lading for Domino and told me where to put the horse until the next riverboat arrived.

"It should be the *Sultan*," he told me, checking a schedule on the wall behind him. "It was supposed to leave out of St. Louis at eight this morning. Maybe two hours if it's on schedule, maybe four—if she stops. You might want to get yourself something to eat while you're waiting."

The river-glitter off the mammoth Mississippi was blinding as the sun rose higher. It was like looking across a limitless mirror. There was a cool breeze drifting over me as the town came to life slowly. I led

Domino to a holding pen nearer the river where the ground was red goo underfoot and half a dozen horses and two sheep—ram and ewe—picked idly at strewn hay. I showed the tired-looking black attendant there my bill of lading and he led Domino into the pen, unsaddling him, and tossing my saddle negligently into a wooden box to one side of the gate.

I reversed my course and walked a block or two uptown and sat at the corner of a tiny restaurant, knowing I would hear the steamboat whistle when the *Sultan* came near. I ate a beef sandwich on a dry roll and watched the tired waitress move dispiritedly among the tables. She was a young-old girl with pretty blue eyes but a constant frown. The frontier had a way of making women old early. Maybe that was the reason my own mother had gone away one bright spring morning, leaving me and Pa alone on the farm. I didn't know. I was very young at the time and had no inkling of what was really happening.

Pa and I had had some good times—hunting and fishing, wandering the woods—but looking back, I could see that most of our lives had been just hard work. Chopping wood, forking hay, plowing fields, stringing wire, pulling stumps . . . how hard must it have been for a young woman.

Maybe I was just feeling sorry for myself suddenly because of the circumstances. I was now completely alone in the world. Here I was, nearly a grown man, yet

I couldn't fit my father's gunbelt nor fill his boots. I knew that and judged my chances realistically.

I was carrying a Colt revolver on my hip, but I had no wish to shoot a man, nor was I sure I could, and here I was tracking two grown criminals who had proven that they sure as hell would kill!

But there was no going back now. I had made my decision and burned my bridges behind me.

The steamboat's shrill whistle scattered my thoughts.

Two or three other customers looked around toward the riverside window and rose quickly, grabbing satchels or duffel bags, starting toward the door. I left some change by my plate and followed along.

Outside it was incredibly bright, but the breeze from the river had cooled. I could see the white speck which was the steamboat *Sultan* a mile or so upriver, its stack spewing black smoke. I started toward the landing with the others.

"She'll stop, won't she?" a worried-looking little man in a derby asked.

"You never know," a tall man in frontier buckskins answered.

"There's at least a dozen of us waiting," the little man said. "Sure, she'll stop."

"You never know," the tall man repeated with a shrug. He moved away, not wanting to stretch the conversation any longer.

"Where are you bound?" a voice beside me asked,

and I turned to see the handsomest man I'd run across in my life. He wore a pressed black suit and a shirt with ruffles on the cuffs and down the front. He wore a thin black tie and a diamond ring with a stone as big as a marble on his right hand. He had a gold watch chain across his vest front. He was dark, had a strong nose and chin and a flaring black mustache. His brown eyes twinkled with good humor.

"Me?" I replied, surprised. "Natchez."

"God-awful town," the man said. He carried a rose-colored carpetbag in his left hand, a smooth, manicured hand, I noticed.

"Is it?" I asked timidly.

"Yes. A hellhole," he told me with a thin smile.

"Where are you heading, sir? If I may ask."

"Why," he answered with apparent surprise, "Natchez, of course!"

I didn't know how to respond to that. I started walking to the end of the landing with the others and the stranger and I just sort of fell into walking stride for stride toward the steamboat berth. The *Sultan* was quite near now, taking on form and definition against the background of the Mississippi.

"My name's McCormick. Colin McCormick," the stranger offered as we held our positions in the little knot of travelers, watching the approaching boat.

"Ben Jury," I said, and we shook hands. He made a little bow with his head, almost like he was mocking me, but nothing like mockery showed in his friendly eyes. I guessed it was just a habit he had. We leaned against the whitewashed rail and watched patiently as the *Sultan* slowed, turned ponderously toward the landing and began to backwater.

Ever so slowly the big boat eased toward the dock, and as the deckhands threw protective bumpers over the side, the sternwheeler nudged the pier, causing it to shudder under our feet.

Close up the *Sultan* seemed immensely large. Two tall decks and the wheelhouse above, the boat was white and gleaming with bright brasswork, gingerbread trim running along the length of the cabin decks. A few passengers stood without interest at the upper deck rail, looking down at the town of Gorse. No one was preparing to debark here.

Finally I heard a slithering sound, a rasping noise and a clank. McCormick touched my shoulder.

"That's the gangplank being lowered. Let's get going, they won't hold the boat long."

I followed the gambler—for by his manner of dress and manicured hands, I now believed him to be such a man—to the gangplank and we boarded the riverboat, showing our tickets to a sallow, uniformed sailor.

Within fifteen minutes we were preparing to get underway again. The *Sultan's* whistle tooted shrilly three times and we slipped away from the landing and out onto the broad Mississippi, the huge sternwheel towing us as hundreds of gallons of water were slapped upwards and over the deck by its force. I watched from the railing for a while as the land fell away, the town becoming tiny and distant, eventually nearly vanishing all together as we headed downriver. Then I went looking for my cabin, feeling empty and lonesome, knowing I would never see Kentucky or the farm or Pa again the rest of my life.

I glanced around for McCormick, figuring he would know where I was supposed to go, but the gambler had disappeared. I found the same disinterested sailor who had checked our boarding passes and asked him where I could find my cabin. He looked at my ticket again and shoved it back in my hand.

"Below decks. It'll say Cabin C on the door." Then he turned away and walked along the deck forward. With a shrug I turned the other way and found the gangway leading below decks.

A riverboat is shallow beneath the waterline and I had to duck as I walked down a narrow, dark corridor. Finally I came to Cabin C, and I opened the door and went in.

There were six bunks inside the cabin, three each stacked together on two flimsy-looking ladder frames. Two men had claimed the bottom bunks and were sleeping on them as I entered the cabin. On one of the middle bunks a kid only a few years younger than me sat with his legs dangling, fixing a broken shoelace on his town boots.

"Howdy," he said without lifting his eyes.

"Is this Cabin C?"

"What's it say on the door?" he asked with dim humor. He was pale-haired, dressed in twill pants, homespun shirt and suspenders. He was missing two front teeth.

"I guess I was expecting some other sort of accommodations. Which bunk's mine?"

"I dunno. Either of the top ones, I guess." He stopped fooling with the knot he was tying in his bootlace and asked, "What class passage did you book?"

"I don't know. I never been on a boat before. I just said I wanted to go to Natchez and the agent gave me a ticket."

"He probably thought you couldn't afford no other kind of cabin," my new companion said.

"I guess that's it." I grabbed hold of the ladder at the foot of the bunkbed and clambered up. The man on the bottom bunk growled something unintelligible. "My name's Ben Jury," I said, stretching a hand down to my bunkmate.

"I'm Randall Hawse. You say you're heading for Natchez?"

"That's right. I've got folks down there," I lied. I didn't want anyone knowing where I was going and what I had in mind. I regretted having given my true name almost as soon as the words left my lips. I couldn't take a chance on Bouchonnet or Twilly knowing that I was steaming their way. I supposed it didn't matter—the ticket seller had advised me that they had probably left on the *Mississippi Princess* and were now hours ahead of me. All the same, before starting on this trip I had promised myself to be cautious every moment and I had already made a mistake.

"I'm on my way to Texas myself," Hawse told me. "I mean to become a cowboy out there." I looked at the narrow-built young man a little dubiously. He took no notice. He leaned back on his bunk, hands behind his head and went on.

"I've got my horse with me, and that's all I need to hire on with one of those big cattle ranches. I'm going west to stay, Ben. Freedom, that's what I am craving."

"That seems like desperate hard work, cowboying."

"I guess it is, but I can take it. No more towns, no more bosses for me. I'm heading for the Texas plains."

At that moment the door banged open and another man, a big-shouldered bearded man staggered into the room, carrying a bottle of whiskey.

"Nance!" he roared out without a glance at me. He shuffled toward one of the men and started shaking his shoulder. The sleeping man struck out wildly with a fist but missed the bearded man who laughed and staggered back a step. "Get up, Nance! Let's play cards."

The other man, the one sleeping below Randall came awake with more curses and sat up, rubbing his face. "What're you telling about, Hardy?"

"I want to play some cards! Get up, both of you. I brought a bottle with me."

Randall and I exchanged a glance. He rolled onto his bed and put his pillow over his head. I did the same as the three men below dragged out a table from somewhere, filled their glasses with whiskey and began playing the loudest, most profane game of cards imaginable.

The boat moved on swiftly and silently. It was soothing the way it slid down river and I would have liked to sleep for a while. I had been up all night and my eyes were raw from . . . well, my eyes were red and raw. I pulled my own thin pillow up over my head and tried to sleep. With the three rowdies below shouting, slapping down cards and cursing at each other it seemed a distant hope.

Somehow, mercifully, I did manage to fall asleep. When I woke hours later the room was silent, dark, reeking of whiskey fumes and cigar smoke. It was sweltering in the airless cabin and I was bathed in sweat. I looked into the bunk below me, but Randall Hawse was gone. Probably he was up on deck getting some fresh air, and that seemed like a fine idea. I sat up, swung my feet over and jumped to the cabin floor.

On deck the air was blessedly cool, river fresh. We were near to the western shore, I saw, no more than a hundred yards off it and I had my first look at Missouri. I watched the deep forests, so dark they seemed blue-black against the bright sun descending toward the distant western plains. Now and then I saw a little house and then a patch of farm carved out from the virgin forest, and sometimes kids would run along the banks of the river, waving and hooting at us.

"Did you find your cabin all right?" a familiar voice at my elbow asked as I leaned on the railing, studying the shoreline.

"I did," I answered.

Colin McCormick leaned beside me on the rail, squinting into the reddening lowering sun. "Everything all right there? Are you comfortable?"

"Well, I guess so," I said with a wry smile. "It's about as comfortable as six men sleeping in a corncrib could expect to be."

McCormick laughed out loud. "Like that, is it? They stuck you below decks?"

"Yes, sir. Did you ever travel down there?"

"Once," he said with amusement, "when a full house broke my three aces." He smiled ruefully at the memory.

McCormick unexpectedly rested a manicured hand on my shoulder. The movement revealed a shoulder holster hanging under his arm. That was the sort of rig you didn't see much in those days, and I noted it, realizing that there was probably much more to McCormick than I knew.

Nevertheless, the handsome gambler in his immaculate suit was friendly to me and we talked of this and that amiably as the sternwheeler swept down the broad

Mississippi until McCormick glanced at his pocket watch and announced that it was his dinner time, and I went back down below to find out what we below decks were supposed to do about meals.

That was when the trouble started.

Chapter Two

I knew something was wrong as soon as I went into the cabin below decks. Randall Hawse was sitting up on his bunk, his arms behind him, bracing him upright. There was blood trickling from his nose and his mouth was hanging open. His eyes were wide and frightened.

Two older men stood in front of him, fists bunched. One of them was whiskered and dark, the other was narrow, and there was a long jagged scar across his mouth. Their heads turned to look at me. Their eyes dismissed me mockingly.

"What's going on?" I asked Randall. My voice trembled a little under the menacing glare of the two strangers. Randall just shook his head silently.

"Nothin', kid," one of the men said. "I'd just go away if I was you."

"He fell out of his bunk," the other one said. Beside the ragged scar, he had a cast in one eye. "We picked him up that's all."

"Randall?" I asked without moving nearer. My father's pistol was under my pillow and I wished now I had strapped it on. I didn't like the look of these two roughnecks. Randall shook his head again, refusing to speak.

"Tell me," I said more sharply than I intended.

"They found your money," he said finally, his voice cracking. He wiped the back of his hand across his bloody mouth. "I tried to stop them, but I couldn't."

"You're a liar, boy," the one with the scar said.

My money! All that was left of what Pa had managed to save over the years. We had been robbed once and my father had been killed in the process. Now I had been robbed again. It was as if grave robbers had come back to scavenge for whatever was left of my Pa's lifetime of work. The little he had saved for life's emergencies.

"Randall?" I tried, but he was in no shape to continue the fight. They had beaten him up pretty good. I squeezed around the man nearest me and went to my bunk. They didn't stop me as I stepped on the lowest rail to look under my pillow. I guess they assumed I was looking for my money, but I had another object in mind.

If I could only grab my pistol . . . I felt stupid. Stupid! Stupid to have left my money in the cabin. I should have had the little sack tied around my neck or at least carried it in my pocket. I lifted my pillow, saw the gun and saw that the money sack was indeed gone. I stretched out tentative fingers toward the butt of the pistol.

A big hand grabbed my trouser leg and pulled me down before I could reach it. My chin slammed into the bunk rail on the way down and I hit the floor hard, landing sprawled on my back. The two men hovered over me, grinning.

"I can report you to the captain," I threatened. My words had a hollow ring to them. I was instantly sorry that I had spoken. One of them kicked me hard in the ribs. The air rushed out of me and I curled up defensively. He kicked me again, on the small of the back, and pain exploded up my spine into my skull.

"Why would you want to talk to the captain, boy?" one of them asked, bending over me. His skin was greasy; his black hair hung in his eyes. "Me and Brad didn't take nothin'. Did you see us do it? No, you didn't. Did your friend here see it? Just ask him," he said with a harsh laugh. Randall watched us silently, the bloody mask of his face expressionless. "Didn't see nothin' either, did you boy?" The man raised a menacing fist and Randall shook his head.

"No, sir," he muttered. "I didn't see nothin'."

"You'd just be making trouble for yourself, boy, understand me? You might make Brad real mad if you go around callin' him a thief! Brad ain't pretty when he gets mad. Sometimes he takes out that bowie knife of his and cuts pieces off of lyin' hayseeds who make him mad."

The threats were uttered in a hiss, but they didn't have to be spoken loudly to deliver their dark intent clearly. I had managed to drag myself to a sitting position, my back propped against the bunks. They remained over me, smirking.

"You'd just be making trouble for yourself, you understand me?"

I nodded miserably and looked away from the threatening eyes, and as I did I saw the figure in the doorway and then heard the soft familiar voice.

"You know, you boys might find you've made trouble for yourselves," McCormick said quietly.

"Who in hell are you?" the man called Brad demanded.

"Just a friend," McCormick answered in that same quiet drawl. "I have a lot of friends. As a matter of fact the captain of this vessel is a good friend of mine. The last time something like this occurred on the *Sultan,* the thieves rode the rest of the way to Natchez in chains and then were turned over to the law. It's bad for the reputation of the line and not tolerated."

"We never took the kid's money!" Brad, still surly, said.

"No?" McCormick lifted one eyebrow and asked Randall, "Have they got it?"

"Yes, sir. I saw them take it."

"Well, then, that settles it for me," McCormick said.

His voice was still quiet, but there was steel beneath. He cocked the pistol he held. "Give it up now, gents. If you refuse, I'll have to put you down and take it off you."

The two robbers exchanged a look. Brad was trembling, his jaw clenched. He looked ready to fight it out. The other crook didn't have it in him, not looking down the muzzle of McCormick's pistol. With a grumbled curse he reached into his coat pocket and removed my money sack, hurling it at my feet.

"Take it and be damned," he said bitterly. Then the two of them stamped toward the door. McCormick eased back to let them through, the barrel of his pistol following them all the way out.

"Is it all there?" McCormick asked when they were gone. I crouched and picked up the sack.

"Yes." I struggled to my feet. "Mr. McCormick, I can't thank you enough."

"Never mind that," he said, lifting a hand. He tucked his pistol away in his shoulder rig, straightened his coat and asked me, "Is there anything else belonging to you down here?"

"Just my father's pistol," I answered.

"I suggest you retrieve it then, and let's go. I have an extra bed in my cabin. You can sleep there."

I had Pa's gunbelt in my hand now and I began strapping it on. It would be a while, I thought, before I felt comfortable without it again.

"I surely do thank you," I said again.

"Forget it," McCormick said, and he sounded almost embarrassed. "I can't sleep in two beds at once anyway."

"What about Randall?" I had to ask. "Those two might come back and work him over for talking."

McCormick frowned. "I guess they might." He looked at Randall Hawse, studying his pale, bloody face. Finally the gambler's smile returned and he said with a laugh, "Come on, then. I won't be responsible for throwing a man to the wolves."

Together we went up on deck. The breeze was cool, the river long and silver-bright. There were a few ladies in fancy dresses taking a turn around the deck with their parasols, holding to the arms of elegantly dressed men. The massive sternwheel turned easily on this downriver run, throwing up fans of white water. The wind drifted its mist over us.

We came to the green cabin door with a brass number plate attached, and McCormick took a key from his pocket. Opening it, he stepped aside and we went into the most magnificent room I had seen in my life.

"Holy mackerel," Randall said reverently, and he gave a low whistle between his missing front teeth.

The cabin was larger than my entire home back yonder. Blue silky drapes hung from the ceiling to the floor beside a long window. The paneling was dark mahogany, glistening with wood oil, and there was a matching mahogany bar on one side of the cabin. Overhead—I swear it—was a crystal chandelier with maybe a hundred glass teardrops gleaming in the light of two dozen candles.

Directly beneath the chandelier was a green baize table, octagonal in shape, obviously for playing card games. Farther along, toward the window where I could see the deep green shore sliding past, was a narrower table for dining. It had a starched lace tablecloth running its length and a silver candelabra in the center. There was a silver bowl of glossy red apples near it. Six high-backed mahogany chairs framed the table. I'd never been in a fancy hotel, but I couldn't imagine one of them being more elegant than McCormick's stateroom.

"Your bed's through this door," McCormick said, leading the way. "You two'll have to bunk up." The room was smallish and there was only the single bed and a dresser for furnishings. There was the same beautiful dark paneling, however, and the coverlet on the bed was a dark satiny blue.

"This is really something!" Randall said in amazement. My own eyes were probably as large as his.

"There is a difference between the below decks cabin and this, isn't there?" McCormick said amusingly. His eyes settled on mine. "Just remember, *this* is the difference between having money and having none."

McCormick proceeded to show us his own sleeping quarters which was on the far side of the dining area. This cabin was twice as large as ours. A big double bed with a carved headboard took up half of the floor. A dresser with a bluish beveled mirror sat on one side, and there was a small but ornate desk in front of the window. His closet had no doors and we could see rack after rack of suits, ruffled and plain shirts in all colors, and rows of polished boots.

"Now, then," McCormick said, glancing at his gold watch, "that's about all the time I have right now. You two men better clean up a little then go forward and find yourselves something to eat."

"Won't you be eating, sir?" Randall asked.

He smiled indulgently. "My dinner will be served in the cabin. I'm having a few people in. After dinner we shall have drinks and amuse ourselves with playing cards. You two are welcome to watch as long as you are quiet and stay out of the way—or you can amuse yourself on deck. There is a public cardroom astern."

Randall and I looked at each other, at our shabby clothes, knowing we wouldn't feel comfortable being there while the gentlemen drank their cognac and played cards with McCormick.

"Either way you like." McCormick then reached into his trousers pocket. "Maybe you can use these. If you choose to gamble." With that he slipped each of us a ten-dollar gold piece.

"I can't accept this!" I protested, but McCormick waved a hand.

"It doesn't matter, Ben. By midnight I hope to have so much money in front of me that twenty dollars won't be a drop in the bucket. Or"—his smile thinned—"I'll be so broke that twenty will be of no use in bailing me out of debt."

I thought that was a strange way to approach finances and your life, gambling on the turn of a card, waiting to see if it brought you wealth or poverty. But as I was to learn, that was a gambler's way of life, and they loved to flaunt their money when they had it. What they did when they were down and out was to remain a mystery to me for a little while longer.

Randall and I went out of the stateroom and made our way toward the front of the boat along a bright corridor. Still astonished, Randall said, "What a way to live, Ben. Just think—all Colin does is ride up and down the river, playing cards, living like a king, buying whatever he wants."

"I wouldn't care for his kind of life. Didn't you hear what Colin said? By tonight he might be as broke as us. It's all or nothing with Colin—I don't have the heart for taking chances like that. It's better to have a little and hold on to it."

"You really believe that, Ben?"

"Yes, I do. If getting rich that way were easy, why we'd all just be gamblers and rich as Croesus, but somebody's got to lose when you play cards, Randall. Me, I'd rather be sure of what I have."

We found an elegant dining room first, where men in starched shirts and ladies in ruffles sat at elegantly set tables. Obviously, this was no place for us so we continued on until we came to a second saloon. It was a neat if unostentatious place with long plank tables covered with checkered tablecloths. After eyeing the room carefully to make sure Brad and his thieving friend weren't there, we found a place to sit, and sat down to order.

The food was more than passable. We had roast beef, mashed potatoes and gravy and grits, with apple pie for dessert. The meal was seventy-five cents which seemed high, but then where else was a person to eat when you're floating down a river? To save the waitress from making change twice, I paid for Randall's meal as well as mine out of the ten-dollar piece McCormick gave me.

While Randall ate a second piece of pie, I counted my change and tucked it away in the chamois bag, holding my hands under the table. I was growing more cautious now. There was a rawhide thong dangling from the bottom of my Pa's holster and I untied that, slipped it through the drawstrings of my little money bag and tied it around my neck which was what I should have done in the first place. Randall had been watching me the whole while. Now he spoke around a mouthful of apple pie.

"What'd your father do that on his holster for?"

"What do you mean?"

"That tie-down thong. That's a gunfighter's trick, ain't it? To hold your holster steady."

"I don't know. My Pa wasn't a gunfighter, that's for sure."

Even as I spoke I found myself wondering along with Randall. Why had that tie-down been on there? Pa had certainly not been a gunfighter. I was sure of that . . . or was I? He never spoke about where he had been during those years he had been gone, leaving my mother and me alone for long periods of time. I realized then that I didn't know much about my Pa at all—and now it was too late to ask.

"I'm done," Randall said leaning back, both hands resting on his stomach in satisfaction. "Thanks for paying, Ben."

"It wasn't my money anyway."

"Well, thanks anyway." His chair scraped the floor as he got to his feet. I got up as well and we went out on deck to watch the broad river sweep past our hull. It was already growing late. The river had a vaguely purple sheen to it, and here and there a bit of gold picked up from the lowering sun.

"What now?" I asked Randall as we watched the river.

"I don't know about you, Ben, but I'm going to try my hand at gambling."

"Gambling. Surely not."

"Sure, didn't you hear McCormick say there was a public cardroom astern?"

"I heard him," I said doubtfully, "but are you sure you want to do that, Randall?

"Why not! I've got ten free dollars to play with. If I lose it all, I still haven't lost anything."

"I don't think I will, Randall." It didn't sound like such a great idea to me. As I had told him earlier, I didn't have the gambler's instinct. What I had I meant to keep. I would need it all and more if I hoped to track down Bouchonnet and Mike Twilly.

"Do you know much about gambling?" I asked him.

Randall drew himself up importantly. "I guess I've played my share of cards. How about you, Ben?"

"I've played some with Pa. But, of course, not for money, and it's got to be a different game when men are trying to clean out your poke."

"Cards are cards no matter who's dealing them," Randall said confidently. "Come on, what do you say, Ben?"

"No," I told him after a moment's reflection. "No, Randall. I just plain can't afford to lose any money. I've little enough now for what I have to do. I guess I'll just wander the deck for a while, maybe go up and see if they'll give me a peek in the wheelhouse, then go back to McCormick's cabin and watch them play until I get tired."

"All right, then, brother. Don't blame me. The next time you see me, you might be looking at a rich man."

I wished him luck, meaning it, and watched as he swaggered off down the deck toward the cardroom aft. I shook my head and smiled. Well, I thought, it was his money and not mine—let him do what he wished with it.

I circled the deck in the twilight. In the ballroom, I

saw through a window a band setting up to play for passengers who might wish to dance. I talked to several of the crewmen including the chief engineer, a man with a walrus mustache named Drake. Around puffs on a drooping pipe, he explained that the downriver run was so easy on the engines that they barely needed him. "It's coming upriver when they start calling out for old Drake!" I went up to what was called the A deck and went toward the pilot house, but a young man in a pressed blue uniform with brass buttons said no one was allowed in the wheelhouse without the captain's permission and the captain was below somewhere playing cards with a man named McCormick.

He also informed me that we wouldn't be stopping again before we reached Natchez unless there was some emergency in one of the small hamlets along the way—like a man in desperate need of a doctor—in which case the people ashore lit a bonfire to alert the riverboats. Barring that unlikely event, he told me, we should be in Natchez by morning.

The boatman told me he was on his way to New Orleans, where he meant to draw his pay and seek work on an ocean-going vessel.

Someone leaned out of the wheelhouse window above us and called his name and he nodded to me and climbed up a ladder to see what was wanted. I started down toward McCormick's cabin in the settling darkness.

I crept into the stateroom unseen. There was a haze of smoke rising above the card table, and a black man in a white coat stood at the bar pouring drinks while two others cleaned up the dinner leftovers. McCormick had his coat off. He wore a vest, string tie and a silky white shirt with crimson sleeve garters to hold his cuffs up. He was dealing as I came into the room, the cards flashing from his fingers as he smiled and carried on a sideways conversation at the same time.

McCormick's eyes flickered toward me but he didn't say anything. I just sort of drifted toward the open window of the cabin and sat on one of the wooden chairs, watching the card game's progress, listening to the stories the men told. It took me a while to figure out who was who around the table.

The captain of the *Sultan,* whose name was O'Connell, wore a spotless white uniform with gold stripes around the cuffs. He had a silver mustache, florid complexion and just enough silver hair across his pink scalp that it looked like frost. The boat's mate was a dark-eyed, dark-haired man who looked almost Spanish, but his name was Wethers, Gene Wethers. There was a Texas cattleman named Hollis Gregory sitting in. He was the big man in a tan-colored suit who laughed too loud and too often. On his way home from St. Louis, he said. I wondered idly if he could help Randall with his ambition to become a cowboy.

I have to admit I still didn't understand Randall's wish to do that. Sleeping out in the open with rattlesnakes, scorpions and spiders every night, riding a thousand miles behind a stinking cattle herd, eating their dust. Just being forced to ride under the hot sun with hardly any clear water and the same poor meal every night was enough to make me wish to avoid that line of work. But it was his dream, and just because it didn't suit me didn't mean that Randall might not like it.

There was only one other man at the table—making a total of five. This gent was named Sparks. No one used his first name. He was thin, blond and tall. There were deep furrows running from his nose to the corners of his mouth, and he stared at his cards glassily but intently. He didn't have many chips in front of him; he seemed to be the evening's loser.

There isn't much fun in watching other people play cards, and after a while I kinda dozed off, listening to the drone of the men's voices. When I woke up it was with a start. Someone had yelled loudly, and as my head snapped up, I saw the man called Sparks standing, his gun resting on the holstered pistol at his hip. His chair had clattered over backwards. He was glaring at McCormick, his eyes wild, his blond hair hanging across his forehead.

"I said stand and draw, damn you McCormick!"

Chapter Three

"**S**tand and draw, damn you!" Sparks yelled again, "or I'll shoot you where you sit." His voice was tight, strangled as if he was having trouble catching his breath because of the anger in him.

"Take it easy, now, Sparks," Captain O'Connell said in a soothing voice. The Texan, Hollis Gregory, was easing away from the table, still holding his cards. The dark-eyed mate, Wethers, was smiling crookedly as if he was enjoying the spectacle. Colin sat with his hands flat on top of the card table, expressionless and utterly calm.

"He cheated me," Sparks said.

"He didn't. No one else saw him do anything, Sparks," the captain said gently, trying to keep a lid on the simmering card player.

"Maybe you're all in it together," Sparks said wildly, giving Captain O'Connell an evil sideways glare.

"Don't be stupid, boy," Gregory said, and Sparks switched his eyes briefly to the Texan before all of his attention returned to McCormick, who sat in his chair easily, his eyes showing only mild surprise as if a party guest had dropped his fork on the floor. McCormick still had the cut deck under his hands, ready to shuffle. A jumble of red, white and blue chips rested on the green baize table in front of him.

"No one cheated you, Sparks," McCormick said in a faraway voice that carried a chill to the ear.

I looked around at the others. I could almost see the tension in the air. The Texan continued to ease back away from the table; the *Sultan's* mate seemed immersed in dark enjoyment. The captain appeared to be offended by the interruption of what had been a pleasant evening. I was not frightened so much as enthralled in a way I can't explain, waiting for the tension to ebb or reach the exploding point.

"I needed that money," Sparks said. I noticed that he was trembling. There was a sheen of perspiration across his forehead. "I sold my farm to raise a stake in my brother's dry goods store in Natchez."

"Then you shouldn't have been gambling with it," McCormick said without pity.

"I want my money back," Sparks demanded.

"No." McCormick shook his head. "That isn't the way men play cards, Sparks. You know better. Sorry, but sometimes you win, sometimes you lose. Take my advice and don't bet any more than you can afford to lose."

Sparks was still enraged. His hand hovered near his gun butt, but he was not going to draw. Everyone knew that the moment had passed when he might have done so. His fury was waning, becoming only self-pity. He remained standing there, red-faced, long enough to satisfy his own sense of honor, it seemed, and then he spun, kicked the fallen chair halfway across the room and walked stiffly to the cabin door, barging through, leaving the door open to the corridor.

"Another hand, gentlemen?" McCormick asked, shuffling the cards.

"Not for me," Captain O'Connell said, pushing away from the table. "That's taken the fun out of it for me."

"For me too," Gregory said, reaching for the ten-gallon hat beside him on the floor. "I thank you for inviting me to sit in, McCormick. Sorry there had to be a sore loser in the game."

McCormick shrugged. "It happens, Captain. Will you send the purser up to verify the chips and cash us in?"

"Certainly, Colin." The captain eyed the mound of chips in front of McCormick. "I certainly hope you'll be traveling upriver on the *Sultan* next time you decide to go. I would like a chance to get even."

McCormick smiled amiably as he began carefully stacking his chips, counting them. "I shall try to schedule things that way, Captain O'Connell."

They shook hands all around. Wethers, the dark-eyed first mate, nodded to McCormick as he did so, but his eyes seemed to be fixed on the chips, chips which the purser would soon exchange for gold from the boat's safe. I didn't like the hungry look in Wethers' eyes at that moment and I told McCormick about it after they were all gone.

He only shrugged. "Everyone wants to walk away a winner," he said in response to my remark. The gambler lifted a small glass filled with amber-colored liquid and drank it down. "It's natural to be just a little envious of what the evening's winner has."

"What about Sparks? He was more than a little envious."

"Sparks? He was a desperate man, Ben. I have a feeling he's been desperate all of his life. Why else did he sell his farm? You see, Ben, men like him should never gamble, hoping to win at cards and thereby recovering their lost lives." He shook his head with, I thought, a touch of sadness. His words seemed often to have another meaning he was not sharing with me.

"Would Sparks have shot you?"

McCormick smiled humorlessly. "Not when I was looking at him, I don't think."

"You aren't even wearing your gun!" I pointed out. The corner of McCormick's mouth twitched slightly, hinting at a smile. I saw him lift his right arm and clench his fist, and when he opened his fingers a little

.41 caliber Derringer appeared, having sprung from his sleeve into his palm.

"A man never knows what the other fellow might be carrying, Ben, what tricks he might know. That is why I never pick a fight." He shrugged and placed the little derringer in his trouser pocket, unstrapping the spring holster from his forearm. "Anyway, I didn't have to use it."

I was thinking that a man couldn't hit a target across the room with that little gun, but across a poker table two .41 caliber slugs could sure do the job. Had Sparks tried to draw his big revolver, he wouldn't have stood a chance.

"I'm glad he gave it up," I said.

"So am I, Ben," he said softly. "The worst thing in the world is to be forced to take another man's life. And over matters so petty."

He spoke as if he knew what that felt like. I supposed he had been in the war so he must have been forced to shoot at the enemy. Maybe he had killed other men over card games too. Just for a moment as I surprised a strange questioning look in his knowing brown eyes, I felt as if he could see into my heart and mind, that he knew I was figuring on killing two men myself.

I had tried to put vengeance out of my mind like Pastor Dodd back home had always told us we should do. But there was no way I could forget the sight of Pa lying dead on the cabin floor, and I would find Twilly and Bouchonnet no matter how long it took me. Would I kill them? I didn't want to, but if that was the only way to find justice . . . I supposed I would have to try, because waiting for the law to convict them or for the Lord to take his own vengeance would just take too long the way I saw it.

There was a knock at the cabin door and McCormick looked that way. Without making a show of it, he picked up the Derringer, palmed it and went to answer the door. It was the purser and an armed sailor. The purser carried a heavy canvas sack, and McCormick stepped aside to let them in.

"I see you had a productive evening, sir," the purser, a small pink man with a thin blond mustache said, looking at the stacks of chips on the card table.

"It was tolerable," McCormick said with some pleasure.

The purser then sat down to count the chips, checking each of them to make sure they were steamboat chips and not ringers. In the end he nodded to McCormick.

"Captain O'Connell didn't miss his estimate by much."

He then reached out and accepted the canvas sack the armed sailor had been holding. There was a sturdy brass lock on it and the purser fished in his pocket for the key that fit it.

Opening the bag, the purser began to count out stacks of gold coins, most of them fifty-dollar gold pieces. When he had finished there was more money in gold than I had ever hoped to see in my life stacked in shiny columns on the baize table, gleaming under the glow of the chandelier's lights. The chips were scooped into the canvas sack and the purser rose, putting on his blue cap.

"Satisfactory, Mr. McCormick."

"Most satisfactory, as always," he said, and he gave each man a gold piece, bringing warm smiles of gratitude to their faces.

"Always nice doing business with you, purser. May I ask one more favor of you?"

"Of course, sir."

McCormick had counted out a small stack of gold coins and he placed them on the purser's palm. "The other gentlemen will be coming by to pick up their winnings, but Mr. Sparks seemed to be taken ill. Would you deliver his share to his cabin for me?"

"Certainly," the purser answered.

McCormick opened the door and let the two men out. I watched their back before going to a chair by the window. McCormick said nothing to me, and when I tried to catch his eyes, he turned deliberately. Obviously he didn't wish to explain himself. It gave me pause to wonder once again about the man's character, but I could come to no conclusions and so I sat staring out at the moon-silvered river and the slowly passing forest.

"Are you planning on staying in the cabin for the rest

of the evening, Ben," McCormick asked me as he unbuttoned his white shirt.

"I don't know. I hadn't thought about it. Why do you ask?"

"I'm going out for a while." He motioned with his chin toward the gold coins stacked on the table. "I'd like you to watch the money for me if you're going to be here anyway."

"Going out?"

"To play some more cards, to relax." He removed his shirt. I must have given him a funny look because he grinned at me. "I know—how can I relax playing cards when I've been playing all evening? It's like this, Ben; I met a young lady today who asked me to school her on the intricacies of cards. Escorting her to the card-room is not the same as concentrating on my work at this table. One was labor, the other amusement."

"I see," I said. I remembered that there were no locks on the doors to these cabins. The engineer had told me that was because one of the line's boats had once torn its bottom out on a rocky bar and the crew hadn't been able to get all the passengers off in time because many of the cabin doors had been locked. Thirty-two people on board had drowned.

"Sure, I can do that for you, Colin. The only thing I would like to do first is go check on my horse." I hadn't been to see Domino since putting him on board at Gorse. I had no doubt they were taking good care of him, but I wanted to reassure him. Maybe I could grab a carrot or an apple from the dining saloon before I went down.

"That's fine. I have to clean up and change clothes anyway. There'll be a little something in this for you."

"That's not necessary, Colin."

"A man does his job, you pay him," McCormick said flatly. Bare-chested now, he was putting the coins into a little wooden box which he then placed into his carpetbag.

"You go along and see to your horse," he said.

I started out then, and as I walked the corridor I found myself feeling pretty good about things. It helped to realize that a man I had met only the day before trusted me enough to have me guard a small fortune in gold for him. Trust and honor are two important assets to a man's character, my Pa had always taught me.

Domino was stabled in an area between the two blocks of the lower cabins. The fencing was white, five-feet high. There were only four horses and one lonesome-looking billy goat. Immersed in thought, I had forgotten to stop for a treat for Domino, but when he saw me he recognized me and walked over to see me, blowing once and shaking his mane. He poked his muzzle between two slats and I rubbed his nose as he eyed me questioningly as if asking, "When are you going to take me off this wood floor and get me home again?"

A voice behind me said, "He's yours, is he?"

I turned to see Randall Hawse, grinning so that the

gap between his teeth showed. He appeared cheerful, but I thought his grin seemed a little sickly.

"Yes, his name's Domino," I told him, continuing to rub the paint horse's muzzle.

"That one there, that buckskin," Randall said, pointing out a rangy three-year-old gelding, "is mine . . . or he used to be."

"Used to be?"

"I'm afraid so. I should have listened to you, Ben."

"What are you telling me?"

"I lost him, Ben. Lost him in a card game. Those fellows skinned me for my poke and then I let them skin me out of my horse."

"They cheated you?"

"Not so's I could tell. I don't think they did, Ben," he admitted unhappily. He removed his hat and scratched at his scalp. "I had a little luck at first, you see, and so I kept on playing and playing . . . until I didn't have a thing left to play with. So I put up my horse. One of those gents had seen it and offered to let me ride out the pot if I put the horse up on my wager."

"I'm sorry, Randall," I said, meaning it. I offered no recriminations. He felt bad enough as it was.

"It ain't your fault, Ben. You told me not to go as I remember. How did Colin come out at his game?"

"He won pretty big. A man tried to shoot him over the game. Called Colin a cheat." I told him briefly about Sparks losing his temper and drawing his gun, but Randall wasn't really listening to me. He was pretty deep in his own misery.

"I should never have gambled with old Buck as a stake," he said sadly. "Now what can I do? I'll make a fine cowhand without even a horse."

"Maybe you can find a job in Natchez for a time, raise a stake, buy yourself another pony and then head out for Texas."

"I guess that's all there is to do."

"What are you planning to do right now?"

"Now? I dunno. I don't feel like going back to the cabin. I couldn't sleep the way I'm feeling. Just wander around the deck, I guess."

"Dwelling on this won't do you much good, Randall. It's over and done now. All you can do is work with what you got."

"I know that," he said bitterly. "The trouble is that I just don't have much to work with, do I, Ben?" I watched him saunter away down the deck, hands deep in his pockets, wondering if I could have rescued his horse with the money I had in that sack around my neck. But I knew that I really couldn't attempt that—I needed the money too much. It was all I had in the world, and there was no telling how long it would have to last. Even with what McCormick had given me it was very little. I had never been a gambler, and watching Randall's retreating back buttressed my feelings about playing cards for money.

When I got back to the cabin, McCormick was fresh-ly shaven and had his black hair brushed back smooth-ly. He smelled of bay rum and lavender soap. He was wearing a silky green suit and a shirt with ruffles down the front and at the cuffs. If I didn't know better, I'd take him for a dandy. A few days earlier I might have, but I was learning fast.

"Good, you're back," he said warmly, putting his wallet into an inside coat pocket. "I don't wish to keep the lady waiting." He winked at me and placed his flat-crowned hat on his head. "I'll have some food sent in for you if you like. My carpetbag is under the foot of my bed. It might be best to prop a chair under the door-knob, Ben. I will be back by midnight . . . I think. So, I would appreciate it if you would hold the fort for that long."

"Of course, Colin. Don't you worry about a thing. I'm not really hungry, but maybe you could ask the steward to bring a couple of ham sandwiches up." I hes-itated. "And a newspaper if they've got one. Maybe from St. Louis?"

"I'll ask." McCormick looked at me speculatively. Maybe he didn't figure a farm boy like me for a reader, but both Pa and my mother had insisted I read. It didn't take much shoving, really. I had found I enjoyed it im-mensely. I didn't figure it would be possible to readily obtain a newspaper on board, but that was all right. Pa had always told me that a man should know what's going on around him—to avoid becoming self-centered, remaining forever in the small world of his own thoughts.

I watched McCormick go out. Tall, self-assured, handsome and knowing about women. I wondered if I could ever make myself into such a man.

Taking his tip, I wedged the back of a chair under the doorknob as soon as he was gone and retreated again to my place by the window to watch the dark river flow on. It was like a lazy, endless dream and I found myself drawn deeply to it in a way too mysterious for me to explain or understand.

We would make Natchez by morning, they had told me. And then what? Had Twilly and Bouchonnet intended to stay around Natchez, or was it just where they were embarking for another destination? What would I do if I *did* manage to find them? Despite my anger and the picture I had built up in my mind of me facing the two murderers down, I had no idea if I could actually face up to such a task. Would they just shoot me down as they had Pa and leave me dying in the dust? It could happen, I knew full well, and what would that solve? I don't think Pa would want me to end like that; he had always had big hopes for his son.

Then, half-dreaming as the *Sultan* chugged downriver, my thoughts drifted to my mother, gone all these years. Gone where? My father had never said. I knew she had family in Indiana, and so I had just always assumed that she had gone back to live with them. But we had never gotten so much as a letter from her, and so I never knew for sure.

That still hurt: Never so much as a letter on my birthday or for Christmas. Maybe, I considered, she was no longer alive. Maybe she had grown ill and gone away to be with her family when she knew the end was near . . .

The knock on the door roused me from my reveries. It was the steward with my sandwiches. Or perhaps Randall had decided to come back to the cabin to sleep.

It was neither. As I slid the chair from under the knob and opened the door a crack to peer out, a boot slammed into the bottom of the door kicking it open, and the gunman burst into the cabin.

The door smacked right into my face and I staggered back on wobbly legs, feeling hot blood rush from my nose. The gunman wore a red bandanna for a mask, but still I thought I recognized him from his eyes. He had his own gun cocked and leveled at me and my own was still holstered. I realized suddenly that he didn't want to be forced to shoot, bringing people on the run. Maybe he had believed the cabin to be empty at first. Well if he didn't know that . . .

"Colin, get your gun!" I shouted toward the bedroom as if McCormick was here. The gunman hesitated.

Now I was sure of his identity. I had seen him that evening; I knew those eyes. It was the Spanish-looking first mate, Gene Wethers. He looked frantically toward the bedroom and while he was distracted I drew my own Colt. He saw the move and it panicked him to be looking down the long barrel of my revolver. He spun and bolted into the hallway, me at his heels.

"Stop, Wethers!" I shouted.

I shouldn't have done that. Knowing that he had been recognized deepened his panic and he whirled and fired at me. His bullet ripped through the wood paneling beside my head, gouging out a huge splinter. I fired in return.

It was reflex only, but my bullet slammed into Wethers, striking his shoulder I thought but I could not be sure. I saw him stagger and trip before he ran on.

Suddenly there was a clatter of bootheels and a knot of men appeared around Wethers. With his bandanna now loose around his neck he pointed at me and yelled, "He shot me!" and collapsed.

There was uncertainty for a moment and then the crowd of men started toward me, believing I had shot down the well-known and popular first mate. I started to defend myself, but I saw they were in no mood for explanations. Two of the men I recognized instantly, Brad and his bearded friend who had robbed me in the cabin below decks. They needed no excuse to draw their guns.

As they did I took to my heels, racing toward the outer deck and two shots rang down the passageway after me.

I rushed out into the night, panting more from fear

than exertion. I ran aft, clambering over a stack of crates and barrels. Glancing behind me, I saw the door to the passageway slam open, saw three men framed in the doorway. I hit the deck and stayed there on my face, pistol in hand as they emerged, shouting to each other, pointing in different directions.

"What happened?" I heard a man yell.

"A passenger shot the first mate," came the response. There followed a hurried, unflattering description of me and the now growing mob spread out in pursuit.

Remarkably, none of them came my way. I eased away from the barrels, moving toward the stern on my belly. I was deep in shadow and close to the wall. I did not think I could be seen. Now I was aware of the big paddlewheel sloshing behind me. It loomed high above me in the night. Water splashed over me heavily, soaking my clothes.

I discovered a sort of cubbyhole in the deck where heavy coiled lines were stored and I took cover there, my heart thudding wildly.

Now what? I couldn't go back to the cabin, but my only chance seemed to be to find McCormick and tell him what had happened. He, at least, would believe me, I was sure of that. I wondered what story Wethers would tell them. Undoubtedly he would be believed. He was, after all, the first mate of the vessel.

I had to find McCormick.

First I had to let things cool down, let them search and hope they'd give it up soon—at least until first light. The moon had not risen yet and it was pitch dark.

So dark that I didn't see the two men until they were nearly on top of me. Then I first saw vague light reflecting on the toe of a highly polished boot, smelled the strong odor of mingled tobacco and whiskey. I tried to make myself small in my cubbyhole.

"Are you sure it was him?" one of them asked.

"I am sure."

The voices were familiar, but I could not put faces to them. Then one of them struck a match to light his cigar and my breath caught as the tip of it flared up and illuminated his features.

It was Bouchonnet and Mike Twilly! They hadn't caught the *Mississippi Princess* after all. They'd been here, on board the *Sultan* all the time. I had found the killers.

At the worst possible time.

"The kid isn't going to give up, it seems," Twilly said.

"We don't have to worry about him now," Bouchonnet said, puffing at his cigar leisurely. "I don't know what the shooting was about, but he killed the mate. He'll hang without us having to get our hands dirty."

Killed? Wethers was dead? I knew I had hit him but I thought I had gotten him in the shoulder. Now what?

McCormick wouldn't be able to get me out of this mess, and I wouldn't want him to try.

I'll never know how I gave myself away, but I knew suddenly that they had seen me lying there in that cubbyhole on top of the coiled stern line.

I saw Twilly stiffen and take a half step back, his elbow twitching sharply. Bouchonnet threw his cigar down and sparks flew from its tip as it hit me on the cheek. Then they both drew their guns.

I leaped up, scrambling monkey-like from the shallow hold, but instead of trying to run away from them, I ran right into them. I tried to club Bouchonnet's head with my pistol, but he ducked away and I only got his shoulder. Still he hollered in pained anger.

Twilly, astonished, grabbed at my shirt and the fabric tore away from my back. I was backed up against the rail when they slowly approached me, one on either side. I switched the muzzle of my pistol from side to side, aiming at one and then the other.

But I couldn't pull the trigger! I couldn't make myself use the gun and maybe kill another man.

Twilly saw my hesitation and guessed I would not fire. He stepped forward quickly and slugged me hard on the side of my head just above my ear and I went to my knees, the world spinning around crazily.

"He followed us this far," Bouchonnet said with a harsh laugh. "I don't think he'll ever see Texas, though!"

They jerked me upright and Bouchonnet punched me

in the face, very hard. Brightly colored lights flickered on behind my eyes, spun wildly and then went out. I was just aware enough to feel them hoist me over the rail and throw me off into the cold dark river.

Chapter Four

It was the cold of the river that saved my life. The shock of the water brought me to semi-consciousness. My head was reeling, but I was alert enough to know that I was in serious trouble and had to swim or drown. The shore seemed a hundred miles away, though it was probably closer to three hundred yards off—only a long mass of black, closely clumped trees against a starry backdrop.

I tried to get my boots off, but it was beyond my resources to do that and tread water at the same time. Now the cold of the river began to have an adverse effect on me. My teeth were chattering, my body temperature dropping rapidly. I struck out across the sweep of the wide river toward the far dark shore, swimming feebly, clumsily. My legs and arms both felt numb and uncoordinated. I was a fair swimmer, but the roughing-up they had given me had taken its toll. The messages from my brain just weren't being translated by my limbs.

The current was little help. It seemed to be drawing me toward the center of the Big Muddy, but I could do nothing about that.

Fully dressed, in the condition I was in, trying to swim was fatiguing in the extreme. After fifteen minutes of it, I felt like just giving up and letting the river take me. But I could not, would not. There was the instinct toward survival, of course, but there was also raging anger in me. It was the anger that drove me on. I could not let Twilly and Bouchonnet get away with their crimes.

It seemed I swam through eternal darkness, but sometime later I noticed a faint yellow haze, and glancing across my shoulder I saw the half-moon ascending, gleaming dully through the gaps in the long forest ranks. It was no practical help to me, but it buoyed my spirits.

I was nearer the shore, I could see that now. I did not see the bobbing snag until I was already tangled in it. The roots of the floating tree clutched at my clothing like the tentacles of a sea beast. The snag rolled heavily over as it assumed my weight, taking me with it, so that I was swept underwater. I bobbed up coughing and choking, tearing my clothing free as much as I could. Deciding it was best not to fight it, I climbed up the mass of slippery roots as high as possible and perched there. I clung to the tree, drifting downriver as the moon glided higher into the night sky.

Sometime after midnight I realized that I was getting close to shore. The current had shifted in my favor. With a little luck . . .

The tree snagged on the bottom suddenly, and the tangled mass of roots rolled over, ducking me again. I kicked away from the treacherous tree and struck out again on my own toward the shore. My boot toe suddenly touched bottom. Amazed, I slowed and tested the purchase beneath me. I had come upon a sandbar fifty feet or so from shore. The current was very heavy, but I could half-walk, half-swim along it's long tongue.

In another fifteen minutes I had reached shore. Where I had emerged there was a bluff twelve to fifteen feet high. A snarl of vegetation, tree roots from the oak and ash trees above me, formed a labyrinth of dark loops. I grabbed on to one of the thicker, presumably well-anchored roots and began clawing my way up and over the obstacle.

Finally I reached the flat ground above and collapsed on my back, gulping in the cool air, my trousers and boots sodden, my skin twitching with the chill of night.

I had no idea where I was, what was to become of me now. For the moment I was happy only to be alive. Curling up in a cold ball, I went to sleep right there on the leaf litter and twigs with the moon sending scattered light through the branches overhead.

Morning brought the harsh glare of the sun and brought me instantly awake. I sat up sharply and regretted it immediately. Every muscle in my body ached. My *bones* hurt. I sat there with my hair in my eyes, staring bleakly through the trees at the glitter of the river in the morning light.

There were no boats out on the Mississippi. There were no communities nearby that I could see, I saw or smelled no woodsmoke indicating habitation. I was alone and lost in the deep forest.

I finally forced myself to rise. My knees wobbled. There was nothing else to do—I started walking southward, south toward Natchez.

After a while I became aware of someone dogging my steps. I first thought of Indians, but that seemed unlikely here, this close to civilization. Nevertheless, there were following sounds from time to time. As I walked I could hear feet moving over fallen leaves to my right. When I stopped, they stopped. Finally I paused, sinking down to rest on the bole of a huge old white oak tree.

"All right," I called, "you might as well come out. I know you're there."

Hesitantly, she came forward. A girl sixteen or so with dark eyes and long dark hair. She was barefoot, wearing only a thin dress of blue cotton. She approached slowly, like a frightened fawn.

"Why are you following me?" I asked when she was within ten feet.

"Who says I was followin' you?" she demanded in a deep, syrupy Southern accent.

"Well, aren't you?"

"So what if I am? This is my family's land and none of your'n."

"Is that so? Well, I'm sorry. I won't be on your property long. I'm just passing through."

"F'r where?" she asked, inching closer.

"Natchez."

"Natchez? You gonna walk all the way to Natchez?"

"If I have to, yes."

"That's a far piece," she said, shaking her head. Her eyes were wide, no longer frightened, but deeply curious. The wind stirred the leaves in the trees and dark mottled shadows shifted over her.

"Is it? How far? Where am I, anyway?" I asked her. She looked at me as if I was the stupidest thing she had even encountered.

"Y'all don't even know where you are?"

"No, I'm afraid I don't. I fell overboard from a steamboat."

"Now how could anybody do something like that?" she asked mockingly.

"Just say I'm clumsy," I answered with a smile.

"Well, that sure beat you up, didn't it? You got bruises and scrapes all over you."

I looked over myself again. She was right about that. I had a huge bruise on my shoulder, scratches all down both arms and across my chest from tangling with that snag. I guess I looked a mess.

"You didn't tell me where I am."

"Sand Point. Just above Vicksburg."

"I'm in Mississippi? I didn't think I was that far south."

"Boy, you *are* lost, aren't you," the girl said with disparagement. Obviously she didn't think much of a man careless enough to fall off a steamboat in the middle of the night and float mile upon mile downriver. Mississippi? Well, I guess a man floating on that current could make pretty near as good a time as a riverboat.

"I guess I am. How far is it to Natchez from here?"

"I ain't fer sure. Maybe sixty, seventy miles."

"A long walk," I said, suddenly discouraged.

"Well it is through the woods, I reckon," she said with a superior smile. "You could at least walk the turnpike."

"There's a road by here?"

"'Bout half a mile that way," she answered, flagging a thumb over her shoulder. "Or," she added just a little slyly, "you could maybe take a flatboat south. There's a few in Sand Point. My Uncle Ned would take you . . . that is if'n you got any money."

I touched the chamois sack which still, remarkably, hung from my neck on its thong. "I have a little. And if you'll take me to your uncle, maybe there's a few dollars in it for you too."

Her eyes grew wider; then her expression changed to disbelief. "Are you lyin' to me?"

"No, I assure you I'm not."

"Yankee dollars?"

"Silver money," I assured her.

"Most I've ever had in my life is fifty cents. I earned that picking cotton for old man Stanwyck last season. That's how I bought me this dress," she said, running her hands down her hips, smiling proudly.

"I trust you, and to prove it, here you go." I opened the chamois sack and fished out a silver dollar. I didn't want her to catch a glimpse of the gold coins. There was no way of knowing who she might tell, and the last thing I needed was to be robbed again. "I'll give you this dollar now," I said, holding it up for her to see, "and a dollar when you take me to your uncle's flatboat."

She studied the dollar shining in the sunlight and hesitantly reached out her hand. She seemed to be afraid to touch my finger, so I smiled and flipped it to her, the silver coin flashing brightly as it spun in the air. She caught it, pocketed it quickly, and her aspect changed rapidly from caution to eagerness.

"Sure! I'll take you there. My name is Amy Drake. My uncle is Ned, Ned Brown. He'll be on his boat. He lives aboard. Doesn't care much for the shore life . . ."

She was ready to jabber on forever, it seemed, now that she had started up, but I cut her off. Getting stiffly to my feet, I said, "Well, let's get going then, shall we?"

Amy rattled on for a while longer as we walked

through the forest, following a secret path she knew, asking me where I was from, what Kentucky was like—things like that. But after a while she fell to silence and we walked on steadily through the sun-dappled forest until we finally reached a rise where, below us, I could see a small cluster of low gray shacks built right up to the water's edge and three flatboats at their moorings beside a long, weather-whitened pier.

I made the excuse of stopping to tie my bootlaces before we started down toward the boats, and turned my back on Amy, letting her go ahead a little way. I took two gold pieces, a five- and a ten-dollar piece and another silver dollar from my sack and put them in my trouser pocket. Then I looped the rawhide tie around my belt and dropped the chamois sack inside my pants. If Amy noticed that I was no longer wearing the sack around my neck when I caught up with her, she said nothing, and her eyes didn't show it.

I was learning caution among strangers. I was very lucky that I still had that "running money" my father had tucked away plus the change from the ten dollars McCormick had given me, and I meant to keep it.

I wondered if McCormick had had any trouble on my account, but I doubted it. I wondered, too, if I would catch up with Randall Hawse in Natchez. I hadn't had the opportunity to introduce him to the Texas cattleman, Hollis Gregory. Maybe Randall could have hooked up with the rancher and gotten a job, even with his horse gone.

Amy and I were soon into the shantytown and I cast all those thoughts aside for the time being. Walking through the tiny settlement with the humidity of the Mississippi morning clinging oppressively to us, we came to the rickety pier stretching in a crooked line out into the river. There were two riverboats tied up. One of them must have slipped away unnoticed. Amy pointed out one of these remaining flatboats, white with blue trim, both colors horribly peeled and blistered. A few dozen bales of hay and some molasses barrels crowded the deck.

"This one here's my Uncle Ned's boat."

It looked as if he was just about ready to leave. If he was on his way downriver, I was in luck. "Should you talk to him?" I asked her.

"I don't reckon so," Amy answered quietly, and I sensed something akin to fear in her. I figured I could handle matters from here by myself anyway, so I gave her the other silver dollar I had promised and watched as she spun from me and went skipping away like a child, dark hair flying free in the morning breeze.

I turned and walked down the swaying pier toward the flatboat. I saw a thin, whiskered man in a red shirt that looked as if the mice had been at it, shoving barrels around, sweating heavily in the muggy heat. From the pier I shouted, "Mr. Brown?"

The man's head came around and he said, "Up in the cabin, come aboard."

I crossed the filthy oil-stained deck to the tiny cabin

no more than ten by ten, where a black-bearded man with a scar across his forehead stood. In his large coat pocket was a bottle of whiskey, in his hand a chart.

"Are you Mr. Brown?"

"*Captain* Brown," he corrected sourly.

"Right, Captain Brown. Sorry. I was talking to your niece, Amy. She told me you might be able to give me a ride down to Natchez."

"How much are you willing to pay?" he asked, his eyes narrowing shrewdly.

"What would you ask? All I have is ten dollars."

His mouth tightened. He stroked his gray-streaked black beard and spat on the deck. "All right," he said finally. "Ten dollars. I'll take it now."

I reached into my pocket and took out the ten-dollar gold piece, looking at it sadly enough, I hoped, so that he would believe it was all the money I had in the world. He took it, turned it over to examine the coin, and then shoved it into his watch pocket.

"We sail in an hour. Don't be late. I won't wait for you."

I promised him I'd be on time, and scurried into the ramshackle town to look for a store where I could purchase a shirt and a hat. That took no more than twenty minutes, and so I dropped into a restaurant, ordered two ham sandwiches wrapped in waxed paper, stuffed one in my pocket and ate the other as I walked back to the riverboat.

I was early, but Brown stood, hands on hips, glaring

at me as if I had held him up. Boarding, I watched them cast off the lines, push off from the pier and man the rudder. The current was swift but gentle and the flatboat lazed its way downstream.

We reached Natchez without incident just as the sun was beginning to set, throwing out crimson and gold rays against the faces of the low-lying clouds.

I stepped from the flatboat without a word of farewell and stood in wonder on the docks. Natchez was the biggest city I had seen by far. The docks were crowded with all sorts of craft: Steamboats with their big black ornate stacks; flatboats carrying all manner of cargo from cotton to furs; and river rafts with back country men, ragged and poor, sitting on them.

The streets were crowded as well. Men and women hawked their goods from corner carts. A wagon rumbled past carrying a man yelling out for "rags and bones;" a fish cart towed by a lazy gray mule plodded down the cobbled boulevard. A woman yelled from a balcony for the man to stop.

Sunset's blaze had faded rapidly to purple dusk and I saw a man lighting gaslamps on the corners. All of it was amazing to me. Though I'd read of big cities, still they had been beyond my imagination. Just as I thought I'd seen everything possible, I crossed a street where a trolley's clanging bell warned me out of the way and a team of four white horses towed past a bus on *steel rails*.

I walked slowly up the street, just another dumb hick

wondering where in the world to search for Twilly and Bouchonnet. Or for McCormick and Randall.

I stopped a man twice my age, but hardly prosperous-looking, and asked him where I could find a meal and a place to sleep for the night without spending too much money.

"There's places on the docks for two-bits a night," he advised, studying me, "if that's all you happen to have, but they are pretty rough. Men've been known to get their throats cut in 'em for the boots they were wearing. Go down River Street here if you have a few dollars to rub together. There's a lot of fairly decent boarding houses where they'll fix you up with supper too."

I thanked the man and started on my way. He gave me a parting word of advice. "If you don't know Natchez, son, I wouldn't wander the streets alone at night."

I thanked him again. I didn't intend to go wandering around anyway. A man likes to know where he's walking, and I did not know this city. I was dead tired and wanted nothing more than a hot meal and a good night's sleep.

Morning was soon enough to begin my hunting.

The following morning was bright and clear after the river fog had burned off. Natchez came to early life, the sounds of the city all around me, bells clanging on the streetcars, high-wheeled beer wagons drawn by huge horses rolling past, newsboys hawking the morning paper, the peddlers shouting and blowing whistles to attract customers.

I ate my breakfast at the boarding house I had found the night before. We sat at a long table before a pair of tall windows where I could look out at the streets and the river commerce. My fellow boarders were not a talkative bunch, which suited me well. I was hungry as I could remember ever being, and concentrated on my eggs, bacon and grits.

The first thing I intended to do that morning was to return to the docks and find out what had become of Domino. I had paid his passage to Natchez in advance, so he must have been delivered. There must be some sort of stable which the steamboat line used for instances like this. I would find my horse first and then look around for Randall to find out if he knew anything about what had happened after I had been thrown overboard. I thought I would begin trying to find him by going along River Street where the boarding houses seemed to be congregated.

If I had to, after that I would check the two-bit cribs along the dockfront. After breakfast I put on my new wide-brimmed black hat and walked outside, stretching in the shade of the boarding house awning. I was still stiff and sore and I popped and creaked a little as I loosened up. I walked three blocks to a gunsmith's shop and bought a used Colt revolver. The mechanism was still tight, the bore good and the walnut grips felt right in my hand. I felt better with its weight riding on my hip as I walked the cobblestone streets toward the wharfs.

I was within sight of the crowded piers when I halted abruptly and stepped back into a narrow alleyway.

A group of six horsemen was making its way slowly uptown, and I thought I recognized a few of them. Drawing farther back I waited, squinting into the sunlight as the group passed me. I had been right. I did know them, but their being together made no sense.

Bouchonnet and Twilly were with them along with Brad and his nameless friend with the big scar at the corner of his mouth. All of my enemies together! Were they looking for me? That made no sense. For one thing, Twilly and Bouchonnet had every reason to believe that they had murdered me. I had not seen the other men before. They had a Western look about them, the way they slouched in their saddles, the way they were dressed. Their saddles, I noticed were Texas-rigged, meaning they were double-cinched.

And they looked plenty tough. One of them was a Mexican with a huge sombrero, wearing a long mustache. His saddle and bridle were silver-mounted. The other was a skinny blond kid with a twisted mouth and wide vacant blue eyes.

I watched them from the shadows as they rode past, my back pressed to the alley's brick wall. After they had ridden past and swung around the corner, I stepped out, looking in the direction they had ridden for a while, still puzzled, and then continued on toward the docks.

The *Sultan,* I was told, had continued on to New Orleans, and when I asked about the livestock pens, I was directed to the foot of the wharf where I could see a row of sheds, a blacksmith shop and pens holding perhaps two dozen horses.

The jetty was of stone—gray granite with a plank road on top. A man on horseback clopped past me, eyeing me curiously.

I couldn't have been more surprised than when, fifty yards on, I saw someone familiar sitting on the edge of the dock, legs dangling, and his face turned toward me.

"Ben! Ben Jury!"

It was Randall Hawse, and he got to his feet, wiping his hands on his twill pants, grinning to show me his two missing teeth.

"Man, oh, man!" he said, shaking my hand exuberantly. "Where have you been? I thought you were dead."

"Not quite." He continued to shake my hand vigorously.

"They say you jumped overboard."

"Thrown is more like it. Why would they think I jumped overboard?"

"That's what those two strangers said. After you shot Wethers. They said that they tried to stop you, but you fought past them and dove overboard."

"Maybe they were strangers to you but not to me."

"What do you mean?"

"I'll explain it all to you another time. So I was right—everyone figures I am dead."

"Not everyone, Ben," he said in a secretive voice. He glanced up the dock and then returned his eyes to mine. "You should never have come here," Randall said, his voice lowering to a taut whisper. "You just might find yourself dead after all."

"What are you talking about?"

"This, I took it from a pole," Randall said shakily, and he pulled the folded poster from his pocket, opened it and showed it to me.

WANTED

Ben Jury for the MURDER of first mate Gene Wethers of the steamboat *Sultan* aboard that vessel.

$500 Reward.

Chapter Five

*M*urder!

There was my name, Ben Jury, on a wanted poster, and I was charged not with some minor offense, but with murder, a hanging crime! My head swam in tight circles as I grappled with disbelief.

"But this is crazy, Randall!" I handed the poster back, watching as he carefully refolded it and stuffed it in his pocket. "I didn't murder Wethers!"

"I believe you," Randall said, his look not quite that of a man convinced.

"Wethers tried to kill *me*," I explained urgently. A pair of sailors walked by, talking loudly and laughing at something. A gull swooped low, plucked a small silver fish from the harbor and winged away. "Wethers came to the cabin to try to steal Colin's winnings from the card game. Wethers knew how much Colin had; he was one of the players. He was wearing a bandanna for a mask, but I knew who he was, and he panicked and ran. When I yelled his name, he swung around and shot at me in the passageway. I shot back out of instinct. It's a wonder I even hit him. I believed I'd just winged Wethers."

"Yes, but . . . Ben, you ran away from the shooting."

"A bunch of men with their guns unlimbered came running. Wethers pointed at me and shouted that I had shot him. They believed that he was the victim, of course, knowing who Wethers was, not having any idea what had happened. Two of the men were Brad and his thieving friend, Randall! They started shooting and they would have gladly killed me. I had to take to my heels. I only found out later that Wethers had died."

Randall shook his head. "That isn't the story they tell, Ben. They say you just gunned the man down for no reason."

"The story who tells? Brad? Bouchonnet or Twilly? Of course they'd tell it that way." Bouchonnet and Twilly would stick to that story and urge the poster to be printed, of course. They wouldn't admit that they had killed me—as they thought—when they threw me overboard. Just two good citizens, trying to assist justice.

Randall took a long time to answer. "I believe you, Ben, but this is no town for you to be hanging around. Not Natchez, nor any of the river ports. All the passing boats will be given posters and they'll drop them off at every river town on the Mississippi. You've got to get away from the river. Or hang."

"What about Colin? What did he say?"

"I never saw him after the shooting. I didn't go back to his cabin because I figured I was only staying there because I was riding your coattails."

"Colin would believe me!" I insisted. "He knew what he had asked me to do. Colin has Captain O'Connell's ear, and Colin and I had been talking earlier that evening about Wethers coveting that gold!"

Randall shrugged. "Maybe he did talk to the captain, maybe not. I don't know if he even got off the boat in Natchez. Maybe he continued on downriver to New Orleans. They say it's a gambling town. Besides, Ben, it's too late now. You're a wanted man, and for murder—they have the right to shoot you on sight."

It was ironic. I *had* killed a man, unintentionally, but when it might have saved me I had been unable to shoot Twilly or Bouchonnet. I wondered what my father would have thought if he had known that two days off of the farm I'd become a wanted killer.

"Ben," Randall said urgently as another group of sailors walked by, one of them casting a narrow glance my way, "don't waste any time getting out of Natchez."

"I won't. You're right." Besides, Bouchonnet's gang—as I now thought of them—had already ridden toward the outskirts of town, probably departing Natchez themselves. Thinking back, I remembered what Twilly had said the night they had thrown me overboard from the *Sultan*. *"He followed us this far. I don't think he'll ever see Texas, though."*

Texas. They were riding to Texas. Very well. I, too, would hit the Texas trail, I decided instantly.

"Ben?"

"Yes. I was thinking, Randall. I'm getting out of town as soon as I get my horse. Have you seen Domino by any chance?"

"Sure. He's stabled right down there. The place is called Johnny Gere's." He paused. "Where are you headed, Ben?"

"Texas, my friend. I'm bound for Texas."

"I wish I could ride with you. If I had me a horse, we could travel that way together. As things stand . . ."

"I wish we could ride together too, Randall." I shook his hand. "We'll meet up again sometime. I promise you."

He looked doubtful, and I thought I knew what he was thinking. Texas is a vast state. A man could lose himself completely in its immensity. That was one thing I meant to do. The odds of me ever seeing Randall Hawse again were miniscule.

Leaving Randall reluctantly, I walked to the foot of the wharf, searching for Johnny Gere's stable. It wasn't difficult to find nor was it hard to find Domino. I walked into a low-roofed stable, smelling none too fresh despite the open double doors at either end and the breeze off the river, and there I saw Domino's familiar black and white head poking over the half door of his stall.

Grinning, I went up to him and patted his neck. He shoved back with his nose and I told him, "You didn't really think I'd leave you, did you old-timer?"

"Hey you!" a voice called from behind me, and I turned with my hand going to my gun butt to see a man in coveralls, pitchfork in hand, looking at me. He was very wide and thick, no taller than me, but easily fifty pounds heavier.

"This is my horse. I want to pay his bill and take him."

The man ambled nearer, squinting at me from under the brim of a flop hat.

"It's your horse, is it?"

"Yes, sir."

"The hell he is! That horse belongs to a man named Sparks. He brought him down on the *Sultan.*"

Sparks! I flared up angrily. "That no-good chiseler. Look, mister, I don't know what Sparks told you, but this horse is mine."

"Got your bill of lading from the *Sultan?* Or a bill of sale describing the animal?"

"No, damnit, I don't have either. I've owned this horse since he was a colt."

"That's easy to say. You talk to Sparks. As far as I'm concerned the man who brings a horse into my stable is the rightful owner unless proved otherwise. So, you talk to him or make your complaint to the law."

Now *that* was unlikely. It was just as unlikely that

Sparks would let me take Domino back. Undoubtedly when he had been told that I had fallen overboard, he simply appropriated my horse. There was a chance that he would sell Domino back to me, I supposed, but it was more likely that by now he was aware that there was a reward for me too.

"I'll talk to Sparks about the mix-up," I told the stablehand. "Do you happen to know where he went?"

"No, I don't," the big man, only slightly mollified, said.

"I'll find him," I said cheerfully, "sorry about the misunderstanding."

The stableman stepped aside for me, and I walked out into the sunlight, whistling as I went. I crossed the wharf, and as the stablehand turned to get back to work, I ducked behind a stack of molasses barrels and waited and watched for my chance.

The sun grew hot on my back and neck; dragonflies off the river hummed around me. After a long time I saw the stablehand take off his hat, wipe his forehead with a scarf, put down the pitchfork and start toward the back doors of the stable.

I didn't hesitate. When the man was twenty feet away from the building, striding toward a small shack, I hotfooted it back across the wharf and in through the front doors of Gere's. I snatched the first bridle I saw off a nail on the wall and rushed to Domino's stall.

Behind me someone yelled, "Hey! Stop thief!"

I swung open the gate to Domino's stall, leaped onto

his back and heeled him toward the front door. We hit the stableyard at a dead run. Glancing back as I crossed the wharf, I saw two men rush from the stable, but they were too late. Domino was pounding along the river road and within minutes, we were heading north along the Vicksburg Pike.

So now I was a horse thief as well as a murderer, I supposed. I was becoming quite a desperado in no time at all.

I slowed Domino to a walk as we cleared the edge of town and the number of travelers thinned to only an occasional passing rider or a farm wagon.

I was reflecting on my deeds and plotting out my next move when a rider and horse burst suddenly from the shadows of the roadside woods, angling directly toward me. I quickly drew my gun.

"Hey! Take it easy there! Hold up, Ben. It's me, Randall Hawse."

And it was Randall, riding a tall, glossy black horse with a new saddle and bedroll tied on behind. "How in the world did you manage to come by the horse?" I asked him and he winked.

"Found him. How'd you manage to get Domino?"

"I had to . . . well, I just kind of took him, I suppose."

Randall, I could see, figured we had both done the same crime. I couldn't see it that way. Domino was my horse, and he had stolen that tall black, no doubt of it.

I wasn't comfortable with him having done that, but what was there to do about it now?

"Where now, Ben? Texas?"

"Texas," I agreed with a sigh. "The first thing we've got to do is figure how to cross the Mississippi. I know a town upriver where they have some flatboats. For a price, I'm sure they'll take us across."

And that was what we did. It took most of the day to reach Sand Point, but once there we found a man willing to take us and our horses across the big river for ten dollars. I bought myself a saddle and purchased some supplies at the first small town we came to after crossing. Then we camped out for the night in deep forest, and with daylight set out for the long ride across Louisiana toward Texas beyond.

Each morning the first reddish flush of dawn found us riding farther along the westward trail. As the sun rose higher the days grew intolerably muggy. We never got used to that weather. Thick stands of pine, tupelo and oak formed canopies overhead and cut off any breeze that might have been stirring. We plodded on, mostly in silence, sweating through our shirts. There were many creeks and bogs, but most of the water was stagnant or black water, and so we rode thirsty as well. I asked Randall if he knew anything about the lay of the land here, he being the one who was originally bound for Texas, but he was vague.

"I looked at some maps, Ben, but I can't match this

to anything in my mind." He waved a frustrated hand around him and slapped at a mosquito on his cheek. "It seems to me that if we continue on due west we hit the Red River eventually. We could follow that all the way into Texas. It will mean angling north, but we would be sure of good water. I think eventually doing that would lead us up to Tyler. If we go on this way, due west, we'll ride into big thicket country, and we don't want any part of that tangle." Randall said all of this uncertainly, and I didn't trust his memory of maps he had seen long ago.

I nodded. This was no good. We were going to have to find someone who knew the roads and the best watering spots.

The trouble was we had no idea where Bouchonnet and his friends were headed, and we couldn't meet up with them out in this wilderness. We wouldn't have a chance. I thought of Texas ahead and the vastness of the land we were riding and felt foolish suddenly for thinking I could track anyone out here. Believing that we needed some help if we were going to make our way west, I decided to sleep overnight at the next town if we could find accommodations. I hated to leave the security of the all-concealing forest, but it was becoming necessary.

I told Randall what I was thinking. "A chance to talk to some people and a bed for the night if one can be found."

"I can't afford that," Randall said.

"I know it. I can provide you with a bed for one night," I assured him. "Besides, I'd like to feed the horses better. Grain them up. They'll probably be living on grass for a long time to come."

Out of sheer chance we came upon a small village just before sunset. We saw signs that read GREENVILLE HARDWARE, GREENVILLE BULLETIN and so on, and so apparently we were now in Greenville, Louisiana.

We stabled the horses, instructing the hand there to grain the horses and curry them down, then walked back uptown through the muggy twilight, searching for a restaurant.

I wished Randall had some money of his own—and I cursed that gambling table he had visited. I was going to have enough trouble taking care of myself and Domino without feeding him and his stolen horse! We found a small restaurant that had separate square tables, not the long plank tables both of us were more used to, and took one in the corner, ordering the special which was mutton, corn on the cob and sweet potatoes that night.

I took off my hat, wiped back my hair and leaned back in my chair to wait for the meal to be delivered. Randall suddenly clutched my arm.

"Look there, Ben!" he said excitedly, and I glanced across the restaurant toward the four men eating there.

"Isn't that . . . ?"

"Yes, it is," I said. He had changed to range clothes,

but one of the men sitting at the table was Hollis Gregory, the Texas cattleman who had played poker with Colin McCormick on the *Sultan*.

"Well," Randall said. "You know him, don't you? How about an introduction?"

"I don't see the point in it."

"Don't you? Look, Ben, we could hook up with them. Maybe Gregory would even put me on his payroll. I could work for him in Texas, you see?"

"That's fine for you, but . . ." I tried to object; Randall was having none of that.

"It's good for you too, Ben. They surely know the trails to Texas! What if we run into thieves along the trail, or Indians? Traveling in a large body is much safer and surer. Maybe they've even spotted the men you are chasing."

"Maybe, "I said, keeping my head deliberately down. "They might also know about the reward on my head."

"Ben, they aren't going to turn around and go back to Mississippi to collect no reward! Use common sense."

"I'll think about it. Maybe after we eat."

The waitress brought our food just then, and I dug in, but not as eagerly as I might have before spotting Gregory. He had been introduced to me by McCormick, of course, but that was a far cry from knowing me, knowing I was not a killer or a thief. I was forced to come to the conclusion that Randall was right, however. Riding with Gregory, if he would have us, would undoubtedly be both safer and easier. I decided to take the risk. We couldn't continue on the aimless way we were traveling.

"As soon as I'm finished eating," I said at last in answer to Randall's lingering unspoken question, and he grinned in relief.

Gregory was smoking a cigar, drinking coffee and talking volubly to the men with him, who seemed to laugh dutifully at every word he uttered. These others were also obviously cattlemen. I assumed they had ridden to Natchez to greet their boss on his return from the North.

"Mr. Gregory?" I stood before him, my hat in hand, Randall beside me and a step back. "I don't know if you remember me, but . . ."

"Of course I do! Ben Jury, right?"

One of the men with him, a slim cowhand with a narrow mustache glanced at me sharply. *He knows the name,* I thought.

"I was wondering if I might have a few minutes of your time, sir."

"Why, of course. Of course," Gregory said loudly— that was the only way the big rancher ever talked, I was to discover. He jammed a white hat on his abundant brown curls and fished a ten-dollar piece out of his pocket, slapping it down on the table. Rising, he said, "Come on over to my hotel room, Ben. We can talk there. Doyle," he said to the man with the thin mustache, "you and the boys go along over to the saloon if you like." He waved an admonishing finger. "But don't get tanked up. We ride at first light."

"Yes, sir, Mr. Gregory," the cowhand replied. His eyes, however, were still on me. Yes, he definitely heard my name and recognized it. Unless I was just getting jumpy and reading too much into his expression. That could be—having that murder charge hanging over my head was doing my nerves no good.

Randall and I fell in behind Gregory as he stalked across the street toward the hotel as if he owned the whole town. We went in to a well-lighted lobby and the clerk gave him his room key before he had asked.

Upstairs, to the right, we walked into a plain, neat room with a curtained window open to the night air. I could hear crickets and cicadas outside, singing a night chorus.

"Sit down, boys," Gregory offered, "and tell me what's on your minds."

Randall, looking around, took a seat on a stiff-backed wooden chair. Gregory sat on his bed, placing his hat aside, and I remained standing.

"What can I do for you?" the cattleman asked, relighting his cigar.

We told him what we were proposing, and when we were through Gregory sat eyeing us thoughtfully. "Well, I don't see any reason you couldn't ride along with us. The trail's never completely safe, and there's strength in numbers as they say. There's nobody following you, is there Ben?" he asked me craftily, his eyes narrowing.

"Do you mean . . . ? No . . ." I stuttered.

"Good," Gregory said, accepting me at my word for whatever reason. "I won't stand for you in a fight, Ben." He shook his head. "I couldn't ask my men to either."

"I understand." I had to ask him, "You know then?"

"About the wanted poster? Yes, I saw a few. Natchez was papered with them. The steamboat did not like having one of their officers killed."

"I didn't—"

He held up a thick hand to stop me. "Colin McCormick told me you couldn't have done murder. He said you were guarding his goods. I take Colin's word at face value. I've known him a long time."

That was a relief. I silently thanked McCormick wherever he was. McCormick's whereabouts were suddenly, suprisingly, provided by Gregory.

"He's ahead of us on the trail. Colin," the Texan explained, "is a habitual loner. And an impatient man underneath that cultivated calm exterior. He couldn't wait for my ranch hands to arrive. He bought a horse and started out on his own toward La Paloma."

"Where's that?" Randall inquired.

"Down on the Brazos River. That's where my ranch is located."

"But, I thought he was a riverboat gambler," I said and Gregory smiled at me.

"I can see that you don't know Colin McCormick all

that well. He is whatever he wants to be at any particular time."

"You were going to ride together—do you mean to say that you and Colin live in the same town?"

"He lives in town, in La Paloma," Gregory said with a comfortable smile. "I live on Grapevine."

"What's that?" Randall wanted to know.

"My spread, boy! Grapevine Ranch." Gregory frowned slightly as if in disappointment.

"Colin," I went on. I needed to know all I could learn about my mysterious benefactor. "You said that it isn't safe for a man to travel that road alone."

"Not for many men, but Colin McCormick"—the Texan shook his head and stubbed out his cigar—"he ain't your normal run-of-the mill man."

Randall couldn't control himself any longer. He had been sitting on that hard chair, squirming and watching Gregory, listening to our talk. Now he wanted to bring up his point. "Sir, I want to work for you. I want to work cattle."

Gregory looked Randall up and down carefully. "Have you done that type of work before?"

"No, sir."

"I didn't think so. Not with those hands."

"If you think I'm too young . . ."

"Randall, I've got hands fourteen, fifteen years old, a lot younger than you. But those boys were born in cattle country."

"Just because—"

"*And,* my young friend, Lloyd Lancaster, my neighbor, has a hand who came out from New York City and turned into a fine hand. We look for a man who is willing to work, willing to learn." Gregory nodded and took a fresh cigar from his coat pocket, removing the wrapper. He grunted, "I'll give you a try. The rest is up to you."

"Thank you, sir. Mr. Gregory, thank you!"

"How about you, Ben? Will you be looking for work too?"

"Not me, sir. Thank you. I've got other reasons for traveling to Texas."

"Oh?" Gregory raised a heavy eyebrow but said nothing as he lit his fat cigar. In the West it was considered bad manners to pry into another man's business. Gregory rose from his bed and said to us, "You heard what I told my men. We're leaving at first light. Be saddled and ready, and you're welcome to ride with us."

Outside again in the cool of the settling evening, we looked up and down Greenville. It was too early to go to bed and there were not many places open. The saloon, of course, was open, and Randall suggested we go over there, though what he was planning to use for money, I didn't know.

"All right," I agreed with resignation. "We might as well."

What I believed, hoped, was that the saloon would be

the one place that I might discover whether Bouchonnet and Twilly had been seen passing through, perhaps having revealed to someone their direction and destination, idly talking as men on a long trail did when encountered by new faces. The saloon had a plain, green-painted wooden door. The windows had only SALOON painted on them in a flourish of gilt-edged red script. Inside it was dark, smoky and crowded, rife with the smell of men who worked hard and bathed seldom. It was also very loud with shouting across the room, laughing and cursing. They had a roulette table, and I saw half a dozen card games in progress.

"What are you going to have, Ben?" Randall asked, which I guess was as good a way of cadging a drink from me as any.

I liked Randall, I truly did, but he seemed unable to draw the distinction between my money and his own. I decided that it was only trifle and gave him two silver dollars.

"Get yourself a beer if you like. I'm okay." I had never had any urge to experiment with alcohol, maybe because my father never drank within my seeing, or because the few times I had been around drinking men, it sure didn't seem to be to their advantage. Mostly it made them boisterous and antagonistic, in my limited experience.

I let Randall go up to the bar alone to get his beer, working his way through the crowd. I started wandering around idly, looking for men alone who might have the time to chew the fat with me for a while if I provided the beer.

I didn't get too far with that project.

Not a minute had passed before someone threw down a challenge at my feet.

Chapter Six

It was Doyle who started it. The thin-mustached cowboy we had seen with Hollis Gregory was drinking with his friends and a couple of townspeople, and as I walked past his table, his boot stretched out and I stumbled over it.

Doyle laughed loudly at his own cleverness, slapping his hand down on the table top. I turned and glared, but continued on my way.

"What's the matter, gunfighter?" Doyle roared at me between fits of laughter. "Can't walk too well?" He turned to his friends. "You boys didn't know that, did you? That there's the famous Ben Jury, a big Mississippi gunfighter—no matter how he looks! Isn't that so, Jury? Killed a man not three days back. Isn't that true, Jury? You're a stone-cold gunman."

"No," I said tightly. "It isn't so."

"What are you then," Doyle asked, enjoying himself immensely, "just a stumble-footed plowboy?"

"Could be." I had changed my mind about trying to gather information in the saloon. Doyle was obviously looking for a fight and he had chosen me for his sport. I had no wish to be involved in any more trouble than I already was in.

I turned and retraced my steps, going wide around his table, but Doyle, still grinning, leaped up to block my path, his narrow face set, his eyes dark and clouded with liquor.

When I did act, I didn't think about it. He had begun to challenge me, still more truculently, saying, "Boy do you want me to—" But I didn't let him finish. I swung my heel behind his to block his foot and pushed his chest so hard that he crashed over backwards into the poker table behind him, scattering cards, beer mugs and chips, his head thunking against the solid oak of the table. Doyle slid to a sitting position, his hat falling over his face, and I walked out of the saloon without looking back at the muttering crowd.

I guessed I was going to have to ride on alone. Doyle wouldn't forget this little incident. Sooner or later he would try something else to get even. I didn't want to ride with Gregory's crew for the next five hundred miles with Doyle at my back. I resolved to go on to Texas myself. That meant I would have to leave Randall behind but he had his job, or a promise of one.

All he had wanted when he had started downriver. Besides, I couldn't afford Randall.

I crossed Greenville's main—and so far as I could see, only—street, toward the stable, hoping there would be someone around at this hour, because I meant to take Domino and ride on that very night.

I had never had time for trouble, especially the petty sort of trouble that comes when someone just feels like picking a fight to show off. The stable was dark, empty, horse-smelling. From somewhere faint starlight picked out a reflection in a penned horse's eyes.

I glanced up to the hayloft, but there was no stable-hand sleeping there; no lantern burned in the tiny, door-less back office. I went in there anyway and put five dollars on the rickety desk, figuring that would cover my horse's keep and Randall's.

I went out again, searching the stable in the darkness for Domino, finding him in the third stall from the back. I was reaching for his bridle hanging from a wooden peg when I heard rapid footsteps behind me, and I spun to find Doyle, his lip curled back, his hand on his holstered gun's butt.

"You shouldn't have shoved me, Jury."

"I just wanted to get out of there."

"This is as far as you go—now."

I saw him grip his pistol and start to draw. Instead of trying to draw my own Colt, I stepped in to him and slammed my fist into the side of his jaw and he staggered back, his pistol dropping free onto the straw-strewn ground.

I thought he would go down, but he remained upright, swaying drunkenly from side to side. Gathering himself, Doyle growled a curse and hurled himself at me, clawing at my face. I drove my fist into his stomach as hard as I could just above his belt buckle, on the liver side, and he doubled up. Then, swinging from my knees with my right, I tagged him on the point of the chin and he gurgled a small sound and collapsed, his knees buckling under him.

Doyle lay still on the floor of the stable, bloody mouth agape. My last blow had knocked a couple of his teeth loose. I looked at my swollen knuckles, shook my hand and picked up his revolver. Hurling the Colt into the hayloft, I slipped the bridle onto Domino's head, gave him his soft bit and saddled up. Leading Domino out past the still unconscious Doyle, I put a boot toe into a stirrup and swung aboard, walking the big paint horse slowly down the dark main street and into the deeper darkness of the long forest.

I swung off the trail and took to the woods. A quarter of a mile on I got down again, untied my bedroll and loosened Domino's cinch, slipping the bit. Then I found a smooth spot at the base of a huge old flowering magnolia tree and went to sleep, feeling sorry about events only because they had cost me a night in a hotel bed.

With the dawn I was riding west again. I saw no one

either in front of me or behind. I wondered vaguely what tale Doyle might have told the others, but it didn't matter. One more story to embellish my outlaw legend, I supposed, and I had to smile at that thought. I did know that Doyle wouldn't tell the truth and make himself look small. It mattered now to me not at all.

I had no knowledge of these trails I was traveling. I only knew west, and so I rode with the sun always on my right shoulder, moving slowly as the trails were sometimes elusive, swallowed up at places by undergrowth, losing themselves in the streams I crossed, seemingly never to reemerge. Where I was headed, I could not tell. I thought of trying to reach the town of La Paloma on the Brazos where, according to Gregory, McCormick was living. Maybe I thought he had heard something of Bouchonnet. McCormick seemed to have knowledge about just everything.

Yes, Texas was a vast empty land, but even out there men had to pass through towns if they needed supplies; they came and they left, but people recalled strangers. Possibly La Paloma was on the gang's trail. Where that trail was intended to lead, I could not guess at all.

Riding into La Paloma would put me on Doyle's course but I wasn't going to spend much time worrying about a chance encounter with the cowhand. When he sobered up, I thought, he would forget the incident. Anyway, it was nothing a sane man would hold a grudge about for very long, and the odds were that I would never run into him again.

With no other plan suggesting itself, with no knowledge of the land I traveled, I decided on that course of action. La Paloma, then, was to be my destination.

From time to time I saw farmhouses but I rode wide of them. Who knew if my wanted posters might have followed me this far? Five hundred dollars was a lot of money, more than most farmers made in a year. Certainly enough to make taking a chance on capturing me worth it.

I was two days out of Greenville and I needed two things: Provisions—most of mine I had left behind in my haste to get out of that town—and directions! I had no firm idea of where La Paloma was. *On the Brazos River,* meant nothing at all to a stranger in this part of the country. I knew that the Brazos is a long, rambling river, and I did not even know if, once I found it, my destination would be to the north or the south.

So I was grateful when later that afternoon I came upon a small log trading post. Six or seven poorly constructed cabins were clumped around it, all of them low-roofed, poor-looking. There was a river beyond, glinting in the sunlight. It might be the Red River, I thought. I would have to find out.

I tracked up along the rutted, dusty road, seeing no one. A lazy yellow dog lay unmoving in the center of the road. It lifted its head and watched our arrival but refused to move for us. That was all of the activity there was to be seen.

The trading post had three or four people in it when

I entered the low-ceilinged building. One older woman in a bonnet was examining bolts of fabric. An old-timer in buckskins sat on a chair near the cracker barrel, and a kid eyed lemon drops in a glass jar on the counter, squeezing the penny in his hand.

The proprietor wore a white apron and blue flannel shirt. He was a short, balding man with a worried expression. I noticed he was missing his left thumb. When it was my turn I began by buying an oversized pair of canvas saddlebags and began filling them with everything I could think of needing along the trail.

As I settled up accounts, I asked the man, "Have you ever heard of a town called La Paloma in Texas?"

He blinked at me as if I had asked him about the moon. "Sorry, mister, I was born in this town—so was my daddy as a matter of fact. I haven't been farther than Alexandria in my life. And I can't say I liked it there much.

"Now, Kilbride over there," he said nodding toward the old man in buckskins, "he might know something about it. He's been near and far in his time."

Thanking the clerk, I shouldered my stuffed saddlebags and walked over to the hawk-faced old-timer. He had gray curls creeping out from under his wide hat. His buckskins, I saw as I got closer, were greasy and patched at the knee with rawhide. He wore a well-used Remington revolver in a holster at the front of his belt and a bowie knife hanging at his hip. He watched me with narrowing blue eyes as I approached.

"Mr.—"

He interrupted me with a smile. "Call me Choctaw, son, most folks do."

"Choctaw." I nodded, liking his smile. "I was told you might be able to help me. I'm riding to Texas and I've never been there. I'm looking for a town called La Paloma. All I know is that it's supposed to be somewhere along the Brazos River."

"It is. I know where it is."

"Could I trouble you to give me directions? Tell me the landmarks along the way?"

"I could be talked into that," Choctaw said, smiling again. He located a corncob pipe and struck a match, lighting it. He waved out the match finally. "You know you're talkin' about somethin' near a two-hundred mile ride."

"I do." I had figured that much out, though I was hoping it was nearer to a hundred and fifty.

"Now, I could describe some landmarks, maybe scratch out a rough map for you, but that's a long way to ride if you don't know where you're going. Easy to lose track of the miles, easy to get lost."

"I can see that." I knew that Choctaw was getting at something.

"What would you say then to hiring a guide?" Choctaw Kilbride asked, squinting through the haze of tobacco smoke. "I work cheap, and I ain't seen Texas for a time." He gestured with his pipe. "*This* town, well it ain't even a town . . . I was just pausing here to figure out what I wanted to do next."

"I couldn't pay much," I answered, thinking it over. I wouldn't object to some company, knowledgeable company, but I was getting leery of trusting anyone, especially total strangers. I did like Choctaw's smile and believed he had long experience in this country, but I was learning that one can never be too careful.

"I don't need much. Some grub, tobacco, coffee. I'll be happy to ride with you if you can stand the company."

He had convinced me, or I had convinced myself out of necessity. I agreed with a sense of relief. "I can use the company," I replied. Because I knew Choctaw was right, I could easily get myself lost out here, and riding alone and green was not safe at all. To be fair to him, I gave him a warning. "There may be some people looking for me who don't like me very much."

He studied me intently for a few seconds and then shrugged. "I reckon I can live with that." Choctaw stood and nodded toward the counter where the proprietor still stood watching us. "If you'll stand the price for what I need, I'm ready to ride any time you are."

He was as good as his word. He needed only a few dollars for basic supplies, telling me he could hunt along the trail and didn't favor other types of grub much. Within twenty minutes we were trailing out of the trading post town and riding toward the silver ribbon which was indeed the Red River.

Choctaw rode a mule, a rangy lazy-looking gray with black ears.

"People think a mule is temperamental," Choctaw

said. "They ain't. They're smart. When they're plain wore out, they won't go any farther. A horse will kill itself keeping on when it should just stop under an anxious rider. But that mule will take a lot longer to tire than the horse in the first place. Their gait is made for long, easy riding if you've got a good runner. Molly here is a good runner," he said, scratching the mule's head between its ears.

"There's no sense," Choctaw added, "in having the fastest quarter horse in creation out in Indian country anyway. That horse is going to be tuckered out after a few days of travel. Indian ponies are slower, but they're tough and stubby, bred to the land. Sure, a big horse can outrun any Indian pony over distance—if he's fresh! Molly here"—he patted the mule's neck—"keeps herself fresh with her even pace. And if you think a mule can't run with a horse, let me assure you they can when it's required."

We rode on amiably, watching as the forest thinned out and the land grew flatter. We ferried across the Red River which was running narrow and shallow, and rode on until noon when we stopped under a solitary, wide-spreading oak tree and dug out lunch from our saddlebags.

"You said there might be some men looking for you?" Choctaw asked. He was leaning up against the great oak's trunk, hat perched on his drawn-up knee.

"Well, there could be." I didn't look at Choctaw's question as a prying one. He had thrown his lot in with me and he had the right to know what the situation was. I told him about my troubles, going back to the farm, to shooting Wethers and being thrown overboard from the *Sultan,* to the little scuffle with Doyle back in Greenville. He listened thoughtfully, smoking that corncob pipe of his.

When I was through talking, he commented, "You sure did manage to get yourself in a mess of trouble in no length of time, Ben."

"Don't I know it." I was stretched out on my back, looking up through the branches of the oak at the far running sky. It was streaked with wisps of cloud and the day was still too warm, but all in all I was more comfortable than I had been in days. Maybe having fallen in with Choctaw had something to do with it, I speculated. I had liked Randall well enough, but he was greener than me, having no real plan or knowledge of the West. With Choctaw I felt confident I would be successful in reaching La Paloma and I would enjoy more safety along the trail.

"Well, in Texas," he guessed, "no one will likely know of the shooting on that riverboat. But if you hunt down those other men you're talking about—they're sure to fight back, aren't they?"

"They will," I said, and the thought of the eventual showdown seemed to carve a little hole in the pit of my stomach. I had already proven to myself that I was incapable of shooting a man deliberately. Bouchonnet and his gang had no such qualms. Choctaw had something else on his mind, and after a long hesitation, he brought it up.

"You knew Colin McCormick, then."

"Well, yes. I guess not very well, from what people tell me, but he did pull my bacon out of the fire with Brad and Scarface, helped me make my way along the river."

"I see." Choctaw knocked the dottle from his pipe and tucked it away.

"You have a reason for asking?" I prompted, for Choctaw had looked away, his eyes going to the distances, and I sensed an unspoken thought.

"Yes, I do," he drawled, returning his gaze to mine. "I have a reason. I happen to know McCormick fairly well myself, Ben. He's a dangerous man."

"He was always kind to me."

"Yes, well, that's a side of McCormick too. He's a changeable man—and a most secretive one."

That didn't seem like a fair description of the McCormick I knew, and I told Choctaw so.

"Oh, Colin will talk easily and tell you things about himself—but only what he wants you to know. Like those riverboat trips of his."

"What do you mean?"

"No one knows why he rides all the way to Natchez to take a steamboat up north."

"Why, in order to gamble, right? Maybe his funds get low and he rides over to Natchez to work the riverboat card table. Takes the steamer up to St. Louis and back gambling. Collects his winnings and rides back home to La Paloma." That made sense to me. It was the image I had of McCormick, but maybe as everyone told me I knew but little of the man.

"You could be right." Choctaw paused a long while, eyeing me closely. "But he doesn't go to St. Louis, Ben. I know that for a fact. Once I was on the boat with him myself. No," Choctaw shook his head, "he goes to the same place everytime."

"Where does he go? What are you trying to tell me, Choctaw?"

"He always travels to some place in Kentucky," Choctaw said, and I just stared at him.

"Kentucky?"

"Yes, Ben. Up where you say you come from. Ain't that some kind of coincidence?"

"Surely you're wrong, Choctaw. Anyway, Kentucky is a big state."

"Yes. But isn't it funny the way he adopted you, like, the first time you saw him at the boat landing? And walking to the landing *where,* Ben? At Gorse!"

"Yes, but . . ." I groped for words, but my thoughts weren't clear enough to organize them. Choctaw had a point, but I could make no sense out of it. "You are trying to tell me something, but what, Choctaw?"

He shrugged one thin shoulder. "You're wrong, Ben. I'm not trying to tell you anything. How could I? I know nothing about Colin McCormick's business—no more than anyone else does. Anyone! It just seemed funny to me when you told me your story. I mean, look at the way he just locked onto you at the Gorse river landing—a wealthy handsome man you never seen before. Or the way he stepped in to break up a fight when you had been robbed. What was he even doing below decks, Ben, if he wasn't looking for you?"

"That doesn't make any sense, not the way you put it."

"No, it doesn't. And then what does he do? Just moves you right into his personal cabin and gives you gold money for your pocket. I mean, Ben, a stranger can be friendly, sure, but doesn't this taken altogether strike you as just a touch *too* friendly?"

I didn't know what to say, but I had to admit that it was odd indeed that this worldly gambling man had done all he did for me, and I could attach no meaning to it. We rested in silence for an hour or so and then started riding west again, my thoughts still fixed on the more and more mysterious Mr. Colin McCormick.

I had the sudden disturbing realization that whatever he was, whatever business he had been attending to, he had been in Gorse, no more than a few miles from our farm when Bouchonnet and Twilly had gunned down my father.

The day slipped past in a stream of half-consciousness. There were only the endless miles, the swaying of my horse beneath me, the sun directly into our dust-raw eyes as it wheeled over and began sinking in the west. We seldom saw trees now, only here and there gray willow trees and an occasional cottonwood along dry streambeds, here and there a lone sentinel oak atop a dry-grass knoll.

The western sky was a sullen, dull red when Choctaw's words nudged me to alertness.

"There's some sort of outpost ahead, Ben. It might be the last place we come across for a while. Do you reckon we should stop there, or keep to ourselves well out of sight?"

I squinted into the distance, over the shadowed land which had become rolling plain with sparse vegetation since we had left the Red River Valley. I could see, far off, a long, low building with a pole awning over the porch. There were no other structures anywhere near it.

"We might as well pay a visit, I guess," I said.

With a grunt, he started his mule that way, steering a little north of our course.

It was fully dark by the time we reached the nameless outpost. There were six horses hitched in front. I eyed them carefully, but recognized not a one, so I figured it was safe enough to go on in. Tying up Domino and Molly, we stamped on into the place which had a packed-earth floor, and was a combination general store and saloon, a long puncheon bar standing at one end with half a dozen mismatched tables scattered around. The men looked up at us as they always look at strangers in such places. We nodded and tramped up to the bar.

Choctaw ordered a beer. I contented myself with a glass of water which was fairly clear and nearly cold.

After quickly assessing us, the men around us returned to their gambling and loud conversation.

"Bartender?" I asked, and the man—round-faced, round-bodied—turned toward me, polishing a glass.

"Yeah?" he responded gruffly.

"We're looking for some friends of ours. Wondered if they might have passed this way." "What'd they look like?" I proceeded to give him a description of Bouchonnet, Mike Twilly, Brad and Scarface.

"No, I don't think so." He looked toward one of the nearby tables and called, "Billy! The young man here's looking for some friends of his. Maybe you seen 'em."

The bartender turned back to his work and I saw a lanky cowhand with prematurely gray hair rise from his table, his eyes sharp and clear. He approached me slowly, rested an elbow on the bar and under my eyes carefully unfolded a wanted poster.

"It seems that people are looking for you, too, friend," he said, and he stepped away from the bar, drawing his pistol.

Chapter Seven

I was standing at the bar of that dark and musty outpost looking down the muzzle of a .44 caliber Colt revolver, and the man behind the sights looked willing to use it. I heard a small but unmistakable sound behind me then.

"I wouldn't start anything, friend." Choctaw said quietly to the cowboy. I glanced back and saw Choctaw's cocked .56 Spencer rifle lying on the bar. Choctaw's finger was on the trigger, and the rifle was aimed directly at the gunman's belly.

"This man's wanted!" the man with the pistol insisted.

"You're not listening to me," Choctaw answered. "Maybe I didn't make myself clear. Drop the revolver or you're going to take a slug from this buffalo gun in your guts. I mean now!"

The gunman who no longer looked tough, but washed out and shaky, hesitated and then his hand opened and the pistol clattered to the floor.

"Let's back out of here, Ben. I don't much like this place suddenly."

We eased toward the door. I filled my hand with my own pistol just in case someone did have ideas of starting something, and with Choctaw leading the way, we stepped out into the night, pausing for a moment there to listen for the sounds of approaching boots. There were none. No man among them had the urge to rush out into the darkness to face a buffalo gun.

With guns still at the ready, we swung aboard our mounts and rode swiftly out of town. For half a mile or so we pounded on rapidly, Molly the mule keeping pace with Domino. Then we slowed and veered from the trail into the night hills.

Finally, we stopped and swung down. I have to admit I was trembling a little.

"That hombre would have shot me!" I said to Choctaw, awed by the possibility. A complete stranger was willing to gun me down. "That poster didn't say 'dead or alive!'"

"It's taken for granted on a murder poster," Choctaw said. "Let's stand quiet for a time here, listen for horses."

We did that, but no one back there felt it worth his while to ride into our guns in the night. It remained silent and empty around us. The moon was just beginning to peer above the western horizon and we and our animals cast long, crooked moon shadows against the dry earth.

"Well," Choctaw said after a time, "I guess it's safe to go on our way now. You did learn something anyway."

"Did I?" If I had learned something, I didn't know what it was. "What, Choctaw?"

"Well, it's like this—the men you are looking for must have come this way, Ben. Where do you think that wanted poster came from? No casual traveler would have given it to the men in that outpost."

"I guess you're right. I hadn't thought of that."

"One other thing you should have learned, let *me* do the asking next time."

We rode on through the night until the moon was fully risen, wanting to put a few more miles between us and the men back there just in case someone had changed his mind and decided that the reward money might be worth it after all.

We made camp on a low knoll where only sumac and sage grew, but which afforded a good view of the backtrail by moonlight. I sat up for a long while, blanket over my shoulders, watching the trail, but mostly thinking. I had gotten myself into a right enough mess. The very men I was tracking could shoot me with impunity so long as that reward was hanging over my head. If I, on the other hand, shot Bouchonnet or Twilly, why then I was likely to be charged with another murder. I was in a country I did not know, riding to a town I did not know. I wanted to chuck it all and go back. Go back to what? I had set all our livestock free. It would be surprising if some squatter or other hadn't appropriated our house and land by now. There was nothing to do but to continue on.

I wished more than ever that I could talk to Colin McCormick. Maybe he could set me straight, help me organize my thoughts, because now the future looked bleak indeed. I would wander the land until my money ran out chasing a gang of armed men who could and would kill me without fear of consequences. I had been *crazy* to start down this long trail. I had felt that there was no other choice, however, and still did. I could not forget that these men had gunned down my father for a handful of coins.

I slept somehow as the moon floated past, and when I awoke it was to the morning and new sounds. A mockingbird scolded in the sage brush, a flight of doves was winging low across the scarlet eastern sky, flying to water.

I sat up scratching where something had bitten me in the night. Choctaw had already risen and gone off somewhere. Molly stood placidly watching me as she chewed a mouthful of buffalo grass.

I rose, stretched, and spotted Choctaw walking back up the knoll with cottontail rabbits hanging from his belt.

"I didn't hear any shots," I said when he arrived.

"Found a rabbit run and snared 'em. I don't waste lead on rabbits, Ben. Besides there wouldn't be nothin' left of 'em but fur if I banged 'em with that big old .56 of mine. And," he added in case I had somehow forgotten, "we're getting farther into Indian country. They don't need to be alerted."

I squatted beside Choctaw, who had started a small fire and had a stick thrust into the ground tilted over it, his rabbit impaled on it. Already the meat smelled good, and we filled our bellies on game. Choctaw had boiled coffee to go along with it, and I drank half a cup of his mud while he drank two. Then we saddled up again and rode on, the new sun on our backs, warming us.

Sometime during the night before as I sat absorbed in my thoughts the realization had finally come upon me: This was my life, this place. I could never go back again. There was nothing to go back to, nothing at all. It was a strange, lonely feeling. I was glad I had Choctaw to ride with.

It was noon, the white sun dead-high in the pale sky when Choctaw pulled his mule to a halt, frowning.

"What is it, Choctaw?"

"There are riders ahead. Look a little to the south."

I saw only pale dust rising at first. Narrowing my gaze I was able to make out the dark forms of half a dozen horses and riders.

"Who do you reckon?"

"I don't know, Ben. It could be anybody going anywhere. It's not Indians, though. I can make out saddles."

"Think we ought to have a look? Or just steer clear?"

"It's up to you." Choctaw shrugged.

"I think maybe we should try to get a closer look," I said. "We should be able to get near enough to size them up without them catching sight of us, if we're careful."

Choctaw agreed to try it, and we drifted toward the southwest, keeping the low hills between ourselves and the distant riders. A few miles on we again crested a knoll and looked down at the group of riders.

"Can you make them out?" Choctaw asked.

"No." Then something leaped out at me and I said, "Wait, I know that one horse." It was a leggy black with a fancy saddle, and the man riding it was Randall Hawse. I knew him by his shirt and hat even at that distance. "It's Hollis Gregory and that Grapevine crew."

"That Texas cattleman you were telling me about?"

"The same."

"Then the gent you scuffled with is with them too."

"Doyle? Yes, he'll be another of them."

"Maybe he's forgot the whole thing."

"Maybe."

Choctaw commented, "It would be plenty safer riding in a big group," echoing my own thoughts. "If there wouldn't be no trouble between you two. We're coming into Kiowa country, like I told you, Ben. We're an easy target for Indians now."

"I know we are. Well"—I tilted my hat back off of my forehead as I watched the horsemen—"I suppose we should see how things lie anyway. Randall is my friend, and I don't think Gregory would let his man get out of hand. Let's see how she sits, Choctaw."

Slowly, then, we angled down the knoll toward the group of riders, Domino's hoofs swishing through the long, dry grass. I saw a head turn at our approach, and a man pointed in our direction. Other heads turned and then I saw Randall lift his hat to wave it in the air. He must have recognized Domino's distinctive black and white patches. I could make out Doyle as well, and even at that distance I saw his back stiffen.

Hollis Gregory held up a hand and his men stopped, their horses milling as Choctaw and I approached. Randall came riding out to meet us on that beautiful stolen black horse of his.

"Ben! What happened back in Greenville? I thought I'd lost you for good."

"I'll tell you later," I said. Randall fell in beside us and the three of us rode to where Gregory sat his big gray gelding.

"I thought you'd decided you didn't care for our company," Gregory boomed in that deep voice of his. He was smiling, and so I figured it was all right.

"I just got side-tracked," I told him with a smile, shaking his proferred hand. From the corner of my eye I could see Doyle, tight-lipped and rigid in the saddle. He said nothing, nor did Gregory about our fracas, so I figured Doyle had decided not to mention it to his boss for his pride's sake. Or perhaps Gregory had heard but was unconcerned with saloon scuffles between two men.

"This is Choctaw Kilbride," I told Gregory, introducing them.

"Choctaw?" Gregory said with a thoughtful frown. "Haven't we met before?"

"A few places," Choctaw admitted with a friendly nod.

"Sure, I recall you now, Kilbride. You're welcome to ride along with us—both of you—if you like."

"It would be a pleasure," I said. I drifted back slowly in the ranks. I would ride behind the cowboys, out of deference, eating their dust instead of making them eat mine. I passed Doyle and spoke to him in a low voice.

"Is it over now?"

"Not hardly," he said, his lips barely moving. I saw that he still carried a bruise on his jaw where I had hit him. There was no reply possible to that, and so I just shrugged and went on my way.

We rode on, loosely strung out along the trail. Randall had pulled back to ride beside me, and I briefly filled him in on what had happened since he saw me last in Greenville.

"Ben," he said with a shake of his head, "you have an absolute knack for finding trouble."

"Let's hope that I don't find any more any time soon." Choctaw, I saw as I glanced in his direction, had managed to fall asleep in the saddle of the easy-gaited mule. I smiled in wonder.

"I hope the old-timer doesn't fall off that mule," Randall commented.

"I don't think it's likely, and I'd wager that if there

were any Kiowas around, he'd smell them in his sleep before the rest of us had any idea what was happening."

"I picked the right time to ask Gregory for a job, they tell me," Randall said, changing the course of the conversation. "It seems it's near to roundup time. There'll be a lot of work the next few months."

"Glad to hear it."

Domino spotted a slithering rattlesnake and he didn't like it. He bounced to one side alertly, but smoothly. Randall turned his head to watch the snake disappear into the long grass and then continued with his thoughts.

"Ben, are you sure you don't want to come out to the Grapevine Ranch too? Get some work in? It ain't any good to just wander all over the state of Texas looking for some men who will earn a reward if they shoot you on sight."

"I don't know right now, Randall." The truth was I had been considering that. I was up against some heavy odds, and I knew it. Six armed men, to be exact— unless they had met up with still more outlaws! Yet, I couldn't make myself just throw in my cards and walk away from this dangerous game. "I'll think it over. First I need to ride into La Paloma and talk to a man who might have some answers for me."

"Colin McCormick?"

"Yes. I'd like to talk to him about a few things."

"You're not guessing that Bouchonnet might be

heading for La Paloma, too, are you? That would be a real longshot, wouldn't it?"

"Maybe not. I know we're still close to the gang. And, as you say, there's plenty of work to be had right now on the Grapevine, and any other ranches along the Brazos."

"Yes," Randall said doubtfully, "but that bunch don't strike me as the kind who'll be looking for work, though."

"No? I don't think so either. Maybe they're planning on starting their work *after* the roundup."

"Rustlers!"

"I have no idea. It would be a good time for rustlers to hit, wouldn't it? With the roundup bunching all the cattle in one place for them. It does seem to be a possibility. They've ridden all this way for *some* reason, Randall. That seems as likely a reason as any other."

Randall nodded, and we rode on in silence until the twilight forced us to make camp along a narrow creek slithering through the dry grass.

I didn't sleep well that night, nor for nights afterward on the long trail. A part of me was always tense, alert. Doyle continued to give me dirty looks, and I had no trouble visualizing him sticking a knife into my ribs as I slept.

But he made no move; nor did the Indians harass us, though Choctaw told me that a band of Kiowas had been shadowing us for some time, and I believed him.

We were too many men with too many guns for the size of their war party, it seemed. At any rate we arrived at midweek at midday at a grove of cottonwood trees beyond which we could see the Brazos River flowing like a long silver ribbon southward, and Gregory announced wearily and happily that we had reached the eastern border of his land.

"That's all Grapevine, boys," he said in his booming voice.

Looking more closely we could see several small ponds among the grassy hills and several stands of oaks, sycamores and willows along the water's edge. A little later the dark smudges we had been seeing grew larger and took on mass and shape and gathered life, and we were riding among long-horned Grapevine cattle.

I asked Gregory, "Where, then, is La Paloma from here?"

"I still can't make a cowboy of you, eh?" the Texan said, glancing at me with amusement.

"No, sir. Not just now. I have other matters I must attend to."

"I understand," Gregory said, but it was obvious he didn't. His entire life was wrapped up in the Grapevine Ranch and he couldn't understand anyone wanting anything else, needing more.

"You ride seven miles north, keeping along the Brazos. There's a stage road that follows the river. It'll take you right into La Paloma, Ben."

I thanked him for everything and let Domino fall

back a little from the ranch owner's horse. Randall had another try at convincing me.

"Ben, you ought to dump all those fool ideas of yours. I know you have your pride, but what's at the end of the trail you're riding? Just blood, Ben, blood. Why don't you come along and work with me on the Grapevine?"

"I can't Randall. There's nothing I'd like more, but I just can't. There's a debt to be paid."

He gave it up, shaking his head heavily. I guided Domino over to where Choctaw rode almost negligently, letting Molly pick her own way, take her own time.

"Are you riding into La Paloma with me, Choctaw? Or maybe you want to be a cowboy too," I said facetiously.

"That would be the day, wouldn't it?" He laughed. Then, seriously, "I guess I'll just be riding on on my own, Ben. I want to see some country I ain't seen before. Don't matter where to me. Don't think I'm deserting you. It's just that I need to be out in the open."

"I don't think anything of the kind, Choctaw. I wouldn't. Nor would I expect another man to fight my battles for me."

"Well, if I could help you I would, Ben. But I got no taste for that sort of work, and I wouldn't be much good at it anyway at my age."

I understood his refusal and told him so. We had reached a small creek, a fork of the Brazos, and there we parted. I shook hands with Choctaw and with Randall and then I started Domino northward toward

La Paloma. Reining up briefly, I watched as Randall and the Grapevine hands splashed across the creek sending up silver spurs of water. I could see Choctaw as well, continuing in his own direction, angling away from the cowhands.

And there I was alone again, friendless in a strange land. I didn't like the feeling, but I had chosen my own course; there was nothing to do now but continue on.

The Brazos on my left was shimmering in the sun, making its sinuous way south. On this stretch of the river their were many willows clotted together, and great, curving sycamores leaning out over the water. There were many quail racing into the brush before Domino's hoofs and a big red hawk eyeing me with apparent contempt from its perch high in a shifting cottonwood. Distantly, a flock of crows flew raucously.

The road I was following was obviously used by stagecoaches frequently. Deep wheel ruts were cut into the red earth. Yet I had passed no one else, neither solitary rider nor wagon, which seemed odd to me, and as the afternoon shadows grew longer and blended together beneath the trees, the nightbirds coming forth, I felt more and more desolate and alone.

Coming around a bend in the river road I suddenly saw La Paloma. It was startling in a way to see something other than flat empty land after so many days on the trail. It was larger than I had expected it to be; the streets were crowded with wagons and horsemen, and there were lanterns lit already in the fifty or so wooden structures and squat adobe brick buildings along the main streets which intersected in a lazy X.

I sat silently for a while studying the town with weary curiosity as Domino shook his mane and pawed at the earth, wanting to continue now that we were near a stable and grain and other horses.

Trailing into town as sunset splashed orange and deep vermilion against the western sky, my eyes roved to the signs, the sights, the faces. Where to now? How could I find Colin McCormick? If he was as well known as they said, it should be a simple matter. But I didn't want to ask the wrong people for directions. Perhaps McCormick, too, had his enemies.

I walked Domino past a low adobe building with bars in its windows and I flinched a little. It was the town marshal's office and jail. A tall man, hatless, wearing a low-slung gun stood in silhouette in the doorway. I kept my eyes turned down and slogged slowly past.

The night settled around me in an inexplicably ominous way. It was only another evening in another strange town, but the night itself felt like a menacing steel trap poised to snap shut at any moment.

Chapter Eight

I found a stable a block off the main street, and left Domino there. I also trusted the man with my saddle. Some men carry them around town to avoid losing them, but I'd rather take the chance than tote it around.

So, in the settling dusk with my canvas saddlebags over my shoulder and my hat tugged purposely low, I tramped back to the main street via a narrow alley.

I rounded the corner, stepped up on the boardwalk and walked smack into a lady.

There was a sudden flash of color, the tumble of neatly wrapped packages all around me and the harsh laugh of a passing cowboy who had seen it.

"You fool!" the woman shrieked.

Woman? Well, a girl really. Around eighteen years

old at a guess. Dark-haired, perky, green-eyed and mad as a wet hen!

"Sorry, I'll help you . . ." I stammered, dropping my saddlebags to pick up her packages.

"Just leave everything alone, you big fool!"

Well, I was raised to always be polite to anyone, women especially, but I had done nothing to deserve that sort of tone. I crouched again to help, gathering up three or four little packages.

"I said just leave everything alone."

"Yes, ma'am." I just spread my arms and let everything fall back onto the boardwalk.

"Now why did you do that? What's the matter with you?" She yakked on and on, and I just tipped my hat to her and continued on my way. She was a pretty thing, sure enough, but she did not have the disposition to match. Someone had spoiled her rotten, I guessed. She'd discover that down the road her attitude was going to make getting through life a lot tougher.

I came to the X intersection just then. There was a brick bank on one corner, two saloons, and a two-story white frame building with fancy scrollwork along its iron balcony that overlooked the street. LA PALOMA HOTEL read a sign near the doors, and so I walked across the street, dodging a horse or two, and went in through the double, half-glazed doors.

I almost turned around and went right back out. The wooden floor was highly polished oak. There were a couple of reddish Oriental rugs with intricate designs. Two chandeliers with gaslights hung overhead. The entire interior was immaculately painted in white. The counter and pigeonhole frame behind it where letters and keys were placed, were of walnut, highly polished, and edged with brass.

I doubted I belonged in such an establishment, and although I knew that I could afford it for at least one night, it looked as if it was going to be expensive. The desk clerk was looking at me. A man in a city suit with a woman in pink on his arm passed me; they stared as well. I almost bolted, but decided I was too tired to spend the night looking around for another place to sleep. I approached the desk clerk who managed to keep a straight face though his eyes looked amused.

"Evening. I need a room. Just for tonight."

"Yes, sir," he answered evenly, "if you'll sign the register."

I took the pen in hand, hesitated, and scrawled, "Ben Brown, Kansas City". It seemed prudent to abandon my name for a time at least. The clerk glanced indifferently at the signature.

He started looking for the right room key, and I said so that no one else in the foyer could hear me, "I don't need anything expensive."

Politely the desk clerk said, "I understand, sir. I'm sure this room will prove adequate."

Still it cost me five dollars for that hotel room! I went

upstairs and down a carpeted hallway to the last room on the left.

Going in, I found the room small but not cramped. There was a brass bed, the linen neatly made up, a water pitcher and basin on a bureau before an oval mirror. The window was open, and I tossed my saddlebags on the bed and walked to it.

I was right on the balcony. In fact, there was a door that I had taken for a closet at first that led out onto it. I guessed that most people wouldn't care much for the room because of the noise on the street which was bound to be terrific when the two saloons opposite closed down for the night, letting the drunks loose upon the town, but it suited me just fine.

After rinsing off some, I took the wooden chair from the room and went out onto the balcony to sit in the cool of the evening and watch the comings and goings on Main Street.

I sat there in peaceful silence, listening to the subdued hubbub of the busy town. As full dark settled there were fewer and fewer wagons passing as people went home to evening meal and hearth. The saloons predictably grew noisier—twice I heard glass breaking—but these sounds were muted by distance as well and they didn't bother me. In fact they seemed to make the town more familiar, friendlier even, in some indefinable way.

It was a long while before I realized that I wasn't alone in the darkness of the balcony.

I had been staring out over the streets of La Paloma, but now I heard a slight rustling sound, and glancing to my right, I saw a woman seated on a padded chair near another door. She was tall, I could tell that even though she was seated, and her profile was very handsome. She was of middle years, but the flesh under her jaw was firm, her mouth generous though unsmiling. She was looking directly at me from the doorway to the neighboring room.

"Evening, ma'am," I said, unsure if that was the thing to do or not.

"Good evening." Her voice was cultured, aloof without being stiff.

"I hope I'm not bothering you."

"No." She laughed very softly. "You are paying for the right to sit out here, are you not?"

"Yes . . ." I started to say more, but there was no point in it. She was a stranger, and perhaps I really had been intrusive. Besides, what was there to say in such a situation? I continued to watch the streets below, hoping I might spot a familiar face.

"Are you from around here?" the lady asked unexpectedly.

"Ma'am? No . . . Kansas City," I said, stumbling over the lie. I had forgotten for a second what I had written in the hotel register.

"That is a pleasant town," she said, smiling now, very softly, a very far-away smile.

"Yes it is." There was a long silence then. I felt

slightly uncomfortable, but it was still peaceful out on that balcony, the night cool, people passing in slow parade. I saw the girl I had bumped into earlier go past in a fancy carriage. The driver in coat and hat was nodding his head as she talked away at him. Maybe about me. I smiled to myself.

"What's your name?" the lady beside me asked unexpectedly.

"Me?" I said stupidly. I was, after all, the only other person there. "Ben Brown."

"Ben Brown, I'm Cora Brighton. I own this hotel. If there's anything you don't like about your accommodations, come to me."

"Thank you, ma'am. But everything seems just fine, and I don't expect to be here longer than one night."

"You are traveling on?"

"No, it's more like . . ." I shrugged and laughed. "It's just a little too rich for my blood, to be honest with you."

"I see," she said, still smiling. "Well enjoy your brief stay with us anyway."

The lady rose then and walked to the balcony rail to look down the street as if she was waiting for someone. I knew I had to start my search somewhere, start asking people, and so I asked, "Do you know a man named Colin McCormick by any chance?"

She spun to face me, and by the faint lanternlight from within, I could see that her face had paled. What had I done now?

"Who did you say?" she asked, her composure returning.

"Colin McCormick."

"Where would you know him from, Ben?" she asked and I could sense doubt beneath her words.

"I just wondered . . ." I fumbled for words but couldn't find them. I am, and always have been, a terrible liar. I never saw the need for lying, and just never had practiced the art of deception much.

"He lives here," Cora said, taking a step nearer to look more closely into my eyes. "In this hotel. You must surely have known that, or you wouldn't have come here to look for him. But, he isn't in town just now."

"When will he be back?"

"With Col . . . Mr. McCormick, one never knows," she said a little irritably, I thought. "Goodnight Mr. Brown; I have matters to attend to. It has been nice meeting you."

"If you see Mr. McCormick . . . will you tell him that Ben is looking for him?"

"Just that? That is all the message?" Her hand was already on the doorknob to her room.

"Yes, please. That's it. Just that Ben is looking for him."

"All right. If I do happen to see Mr. McCormick, I'll tell him."

"Ma'am," I said before she went inside. "It was nice meeting you too."

She nodded, offered me a parting smile which she didn't seem to quite mean, and then swept inside. I heard the door lock behind her and I shrugged mentally and returned to my street-watching.

That had been a strange encounter, I reflected. One thing was obvious—she knew McCormick. Knew him pretty well. I remembered her starting to use his first name automatically. Also, I was sure, she did not believe that my name was Ben Brown. Had McCormick, then, mentioned me to her? I didn't know, but all in all it had been an odd conversation, with much more unsaid than said.

I yawned and rose, picking up my chair. I was very tired. The trail had been a long one. All the same, I was going to go out somewhere and buy myself a big steak dinner before giving up the day.

Morning dawned bright and crisp. There was frost on the sundown side of the hills and in the shadows under the trees. I had risen early out of habit, saddled Domino and ridden out of town, going nowhere, getting the lay of the land, letting my mind wander. I found a grassy dell with scattered pinyon pines and live oaks and swung down for a time to let Domino graze and to allow my thoughts to run free.

I had begun to question myself about several matters. I might have been wrong about several things, I decided. Was I so sure that McCormick would be glad to see me again? Maybe I had been nothing more than a nuisance to him back on the river, and would be the same here in La Paloma. Also, I still did not really know who, *what,* McCormick was. Choctaw Kilbride, Hollis Gregory and the lady at the hotel, Cora Brighton all seemed to know a different Colin McCormick than I did.

The truth was, I decided, I didn't need to see McCormick and there was no particular reason why he should be happy to see me again. To him I was undoubtedly nothing more than a casual acquaintance, our paths briefly crossing.

Except—why? Why had he been in Kentucky, not only in Kentucky, but in Gorse? Choctaw had told me he was often there. *Why?* I didn't want to inquire about that if we did ever meet again although I was deeply curious. It was probably none of my business and would likely be viewed as prying into matters that didn't concern me in the least. After all, if he'd wanted to tell me, there had been time on the riverboat.

"Let's go, Domino," I said, swinging aboard again. I would just forget about Colin McCormick, I thought. I was on my own; might as well face it. There was no sense waiting for McCormick or anyone else to help me find Bouchonnet and Twilly and see that justice was done.

Justice. That was another issue. Let's say I could capture Twilly and Bouchonnet somehow. Then what? Take them to the marshal without a shred of proof against them? I'd probably get myself arrested. They were undoubtedly carrying around another wanted poster just for protection in case they wished to kill me. It was too much for me to solve. Briefly I wished that I had just ridden on with Choctaw, going nowhere. But could my father ever have forgiven a son who would cut and run? Could I ever forgive myself if I didn't at least try to see that justice was served?

"Hello!" There was no one in the stable when I returned to La Paloma, which seemed odd. It was still early morning. I led Domino back to the stall he had occupied overnight and put him in it, unsaddling.

"Still got that little money sack?" someone said behind me, and I spun, saddle in hands, to see Brad, the bearded thug, standing there, revolver drawn. He grinned crookedly at me.

"You never know when people will show up, do you?" he asked sarcastically.

"It seems not." I was trying to think, but my head was racing with singing blood. I couldn't drop the saddle and go for my gun, nor throw it at him. He was too far away. He had the drop on me, and that was that. I took Brad for a bully and a thief, but not a cold-blooded killer. Maybe, I thought, I could still profit from this situation.

"I thought you were riding with Bouchonnet, Brad."

"Did you? You know his name, then, do you?"

"We've met." I tried to keep my voice light.

"Have you? Funny, I sort of got the idea that you wanted to kill him."

"Where'd you get that idea?" I asked with an artificial smile.

"From Bouchonnet, where do you think," he snapped, his smile disappearing. "You toss me that gold sack of yours, Jury, and I'll leave you alone. I ain't a killer unless I have to be."

"All right, Brad. Watch that trigger finger now. I don't want to be killed either." I slowly put the saddle down and reached inside my shirt with my left hand. I thought I could do it now—throw myself to one side, draw my gun as I moved . . .

My leg muscles tensed for the maneuver and I started to move, to roll under Domino and draw my Colt. Before I could make the attempt I heard a sound behind me. The scuffing of boot leather against the stable floor.

Stupid! Of course Scarface would be there if Brad was bent on sticking me up. The two always traveled together. That was as far as my wild thoughts got. I saw Scarface's shadow as he rushed at me from behind, saw something flicking down toward my head and then the barrel of his pistol slammed into my skull just over my ear and I went down, spinning away into some dark silent abyss.

When I came around it was to a world bathed in confusion. I couldn't tell if I was upside down or right side up. I opened my eyes and the world slipped out from under me, spinning crazily away. I shut my eyes again, struggling to find a mental compass while little men with big hammers pounded away inside my skull.

After a long, long while I sat up. Automatically I looked for my chamois sack. It was gone of course. The real surprise would have been to find it untouched. I rubbed my neck. It burned where the rawhide tie had been ripped from it.

I heard someone walking slowly past the stall and I peered up through the murkiness of my vision and said, "Can you help me?"

"Huh." The footsteps returned and I saw the tall, rail-thin stablehand standing over me, looking worried and nervous.

"What happened? Your horse kick you?"

"Two men jumped me and robbed me. Help me up, will you please?"

"Sure." He looked around anxiously, reassuring himself that my attackers had gone, then he hooked his hands under both of my arms and together we managed to get me more or less upright. I leaned against the partition of the stall, my elbow hooked over it for support.

"We ought to get the marshal! Did you see who it was?"

"No," I lied, "I didn't see them. It wouldn't do any good to get the marshal." Quite the opposite, if he asked me who I was.

"He should be told," the stablehand said, disagreeing. "We don't want the stable involved in this kind of mess."

"It won't be," I reassured him, "and I'm *not* going to report this, so no one can blame you for anything. I'll take care of this matter in my own way."

"Well . . ." He looked doubtful, but he was a man used to letting others make his decisions for him, so in the end he just shrugged and agreed. "As you say. I think you better come out back, let me pump some water over your head."

That much I gratefully let the man do for me. I stripped off my shirt and hung my aching head under the water spout. In a few minutes the water gushed out, icy cold. It numbed me all the way down my spine, but cleared my head a little. I straightened up, wiping back my hair. The stablehand ducked inside and returned with a none-too-clean towel.

I dug into my jeans and found something thin and hard. I withdrew it and grinned weakly. "They must have missed this. I've got five dollars left to my name, so I'll be leaving my horse again. Maybe overnight too. I can't be sure yet. I'd appreciate it if you'd grain him up and rub him down good, will you do that?"

"Sure thing, mister," he said as I gave him the last money I had in the world. "And," I warned him, "you make sure you watch that animal, friend. Don't let anyone get near that horse. He's all I own now." My manner was grim and he understood me.

"I got a scattergun inside. I believe I just might keep it close at hand the rest of the day."

"Good." I put a hand on his scrawny shoulder. "Thanks a lot."

Then I walked away, using the alley. I was determined to find a couple of men. This time if they want-ed me, they would have to try it face to face.

Anger impelled me as I wandered through the town. Slowly, as the sun rose high and the day grew hot, my anger ebbed, but my determination did not. I was going to find the two robbers if they were still in La Paloma. After a while I was forced to come to the unhappy conclusion that they were not. I supposed it would have been unusual for them to rob someone and then simply hang around to see what happened next. No, Brad and Scarface were long gone.

I sat on a shady bench in front of the bank and stared uptown. I had to face it, my money was gone and so were the thieves.

Now what?

Now what indeed. To be friendless and broke in a strange town is no cheering predicament. I had Domino and the supplies in my saddlebags. Nothing else.

There was a sudden uproar down the street to my left. A stagecoach was pulling in, dragging a veil of hot dust behind it, and a group of men was rushing that way. I could see the shotgun rider slumped over in the box. As curious as everyone else, I started that way.

"Hit us just past Devil Crossing," the stagecoach driver was saying.

"How many, Hank?"

"Just the one. A tall man." The driver wiped sweat from his eyes.

"Did you see his face?"

"No, damit! Give me a hand down, boys, and help me get Charlie to the doctor, this ain't no time for talking."

This conversation was all shouted, one sentence on top of the last. Now the men fell to silence and looked in my direction, and I turned to see the tall man with the handlebar mustache, silver star gleaming on his striped cotton vest, striding toward the stage station. I withdrew from the crowd a little. Not that the marshal had time to worry about me just then, but I wished to stay as far away from him as possible while in town.

From what I could gather from the loud disjointed conversation a lone rider had stopped the stage and demanded the strongbox. The shotgun rider, Charlie, had tried to throw down on the outlaw and been shot for his trouble.

That was about it. A little man in a tan town suit was buzzing around, wringing his hands. I guess he was in charge of the La Paloma stage station. The marshal was talking quietly with the stage driver, and two men supporting Charlie started toward the doctor's office up the street.

Slowly the crowd began to break up and drift away toward the saloons where they could discuss the news in depth. I drifted as well. I had been thinking, of course, that Bouchonnet's and Twilly's gang might have something to do with the stickup, but Brad and Scarface could hardly have been in two places at once, and why would they have come looking for my small purse if they had a big job planned? There was that, and they had said that it was only a single robber who had stopped the stagecoach.

I tossed those thoughts carelessly aside. I had my own worries and they had nothing to do with a road agent.

Or so I believed at the time.

Continuing on my way, I stepped up onto the board-walk and paused briefly as I tried to decide which course to take from there, when I just happened to overhear a conversation between two older men on the corner.

"In broad daylight!" one of them was saying. "Who says things are getting more civilized around here? Why it's getting worse and worse. The marshal don't seem able to do a damn thing about it."

"Well, Walt, it ain't all the marshal's fault," the second man said.

"I realize that, but we never would've had this kind of lawlessness back when Fred Jury was marshal. They didn't fool with old Fred, no sir!"

I turned my head slowly toward the two men, my mouth open silently. I felt stunned, more deeply puzzled than ever. Nothing in my world seemed to stay rooted to one place lately. Everything that I believed I knew kept falling apart and forming itself into new riddles.

When Fred Jury was marshal . . .

And Fred Jury had been my father.

Chapter Nine

I rode slowly through the oak-studded hills. The shadows beneath the trees were already deep. A red-tailed hawk swung in lazy circles high above me. Domino moved on easily, steadily over the dry grass countryside.

I was riding slowly, not eager to arrive at my destination. I had realized earlier that I had almost nowhere left to go, and so broke and despondent, I rode toward Hollis Gregory's Grapevine Ranch. There, at least, I had a friend or two and they would give me meals and a roof over my head. There, at least, I could earn some money.

I smiled without humor—a dollar a day was the going wage for a new-hire cowhand. How long would it take to replace what I had lost to Brad and Scarface? If I was to work for Gregory, how could I pursue my father's killers? Yet without any money at all, how far could I travel on anyway? I was in a fair fix, that was for sure, and this was the only solution I could come up with.

I had come so far and learned so little. Where was Colin McCormick, and *what* was he?

And! Who had Fred Jury been? Why had my father never told me that he had been a lawman. It explained certain small things, like the tie-down on his holster. It wasn't only outlaws that tie their guns down in order to draw straight and smooth.

I had begun to wonder if his murder had something to do with his past career as a lawman. After all, hadn't Bouchonnet and Twilly ridden right back to La Paloma after the killing?

I should have hung around in town, I supposed, talking to people about Fred Jury, but with the wanted poster out on me it wasn't wise to stay too near the marshal. Kent was his name, I had discovered. Alvin Kent. Mostly people seemed to think he was honest. But mostly they didn't think him capable of doing his job well. The stagecoach robbery today was apparently one in a long line of thefts, shootings and rustling crimes committed on his watch.

"The outlaws around here give us more trouble than the Kiowas ever did," I heard one old-timer say. It seemed there was mounting pressure on Marshal Kent to get La Paloma cleaned up. I sure didn't want to be the scapegoat for all of his troubles. Me—murderer, horse thief. Ben Jury! Son of a marshal who turned out to be a bad one.

I rode on slowly. A quail called and another answered in the blackjack thicket I passed. Now I could see smoke rising from a distant chimney, curling against a darkening sky. Far to the east I could make out a single star already glittering against the deep velvet of approaching night.

I crested a rise and found myself suddenly looking down at the Grapevine Ranch house.

Long and white, Gregory's house had two verandas. Two big elm trees grew at either side of the veranda on the north side of the house, the front. Beyond the big house I could see several outbuildings—a blacksmith's shed, smokehouse and tack shed, most likely, and farther on, toward the Brazos River glowing a bluish silver in the twilight, a long building I took for the bunkhouse. To one side of the house and back a hundred feet or so was a large white barn with a green shingled roof. Beside that was a half-acre corral of white-painted poles. Only half a dozen horses stood there. In a neighboring smaller pen there was a huge red bull.

I started on down the slope toward the main house, wishing still that there was some other path for me to follow. Slowly I walked Domino to the hitchrail before the front door and sat there for a long minute before swinging down, stepping up onto the porch where I knocked and waited, hat in hand like any drifting cowhand.

Gregory himself opened the door. He wore a white

shirt and string tie but no coat. His silver hair was brushed back. His eyes narrowed at first, but then a smile parted his lips.

"Well!" he said loudly. "The wanderer returns."

"It looks that way, sir," I said with some embarrassment.

"Who is it, Father?" I heard a female voice call from inside the house.

"Business, honey!" Then he turned back to me.

"We have some people over, Ben. The Lancasters from across the river and the school teacher. Maybe if you'd go around to the back door and wait there for a minute, we could talk."

Hollis looked a little sheepish as he made his request, but I understood. Riding the trail with me was not quite the same as inviting me into the parlor when dress-up company was there.

I walked around to the back door, walking Domino along behind me. I don't know who was cooking inside the kitchen, but I could smell beef, cornmeal, salsa and frijoles all blended together. Tamales? That was my first guess. With beans on the side. I was making myself hungry, thinking about it. I waited around the back door which led directly into the kitchen beyond, listening for a few minutes to the clatter of pots and pans and rushed voices speaking Spanish.

Gregory appeared suddenly, a glass of whiskey in his hand. He glanced behind him and stepped out into the night.

"So, what is it I can do for you, Ben? A job?"

"Yes, sir."

"That's what I figured. Tell me this first—can you get along with Doyle?"

"So long as he will try to get along with me, sir," I answered and Hollis nodded. The story of the fight had obviously gotten out.

"I won't stand for any fighting on my place," he said. "Anything like that and both of you are going to be sent down the road, roundup or not."

"I understand, Mr. Gregory. As far as I'm concerned it's over."

He studied me by the rectangle of light falling through the window onto the yard. "All right," he said finally, "I believe you, Ben. Most of the boys are out on roundup just now. Staying in line shacks. I know you haven't worked cattle before . . ." At the negative shake of my head, he added, "But I can use a yard hand. It'll mean chopping wood, carrying water, mending corral fences. All the things a regular cowboy hates to do because it can't be done from horseback," he finished with a smile.

"It would suit me, Mr. Gregory. I'd be pleased to do it."

"All right then. It's true that it's hard to find a good man to do the yard. Most of my hands think it's work only suited for an old-timer. Really, I think they just like the freedom of working the herds, and I can understand that. So if you'll go along to the bunkhouse there," he said indicating the building I had spotted earlier, "and tell Doc Parson that I sent you, he'll see that you're fed and given a bunk, and get you started in the morning. Show you where the tools are and such."

"All right. I thank you sincerely, Mr. Gregory," I said, and we shook hands

The kitchen door opened behind him and bright light tumbled out. "Father," the girl said, "for goodness' sake. You do have company in the parlor!"

I felt my mouth go dry. I swallowed hard and stared. The young woman stared back at me, not happily. She was Gregory's daughter. And the girl I had bumped into in La Paloma, scattering her packages.

"What are you doing here?" she demanded harshly. Gregory was startled at her tone of voice.

"Susan!" he admonished. Then to me, "Do you two know each other?"

"Not really."

"This is the clumsy oaf who ran into me in town and then just threw my packages down on the ground," Susan Gregory said with heat.

"I'm sorry I bumped into you. I apologized then; I'll do so again."

"You *threw* my packages down on the ground!" she said, containing a shriek, but just barely—out of deference to the guests inside the house, I guessed. Now it was Gregory who had to remind her that they did have company.

"We must get back to our guests, Susan."

"You just threw my things down!" Susan persisted.

"I bumped into you accidentally. You told me to leave everything alone, and so I did."

I thought Gregory was smiling, but the expression was so thin that it was hard to be sure. I was hoping that this encounter wasn't going to ruin my chance of getting the job I really needed.

"What is he doing here, if I may ask?" Susan said to her father. Her fisted hands were on her hips, her head cocked challengingly.

"I've just hired Ben as yard hand. I know him. If you two don't like each other—stay away from each other. That's simple, isn't it? Come now, Susan, we do have guests. And, Ben, you can—"

"Yes, sir." I swung aboard Domino and turned him instantly toward the bunkhouse. I was on the move before Gregory had gotten his firebrand daughter back inside the house. I had been right about one thing—she was a pretty girl, very pretty in that white dress with its puffed sleeves, dark hair pinned up and decorated with pearls or something like that. And she smelled so sweetly of jasmine . . .

But, Lord, was she mean!

Reaching the front of the bunkhouse, I swung down. There were no other horses tied to the hitchrail. Most everyone appeared to be out on the range as I had been told. Tramping inside I hesitated, saddlebags over my shoulder, then rapped on the open door, looking along an empty room. There were eight bunks in there. From outside the entire log structure seemed to be of a piece.

Now I could see that it was divided into two separate bunkhouses with a kitchen in the middle.

Walking that way, I found the kitchen, too, was empty. Proceeding through to the other bunkhouse where eight more bunks stood, I saw a man sitting on a bunk, sewing a button on his shirt.

"Are you Doc Parson?"

"I am. I admit it."

"Fine. Doc, Mr. Gregory told me you'd get me fixed up with some grub and a bunk and get me lined out for tomorrow. I'm the new yard hand."

Doc placed his shirt aside and rose from the bunk. He was white-haired, going bald, and his shoulders were hunched, but his gnarled hand shook mine firmly.

"What'd you say your name was?"

Well, there were half a dozen people on the Grapevine who already knew my real name and there was no sense pretending, so I owned up to it. "My name is Ben Jury."

"Jury?" Doc scratched his head, pondering. "Name sounds familiar somehow."

"I'm a friend of Randall Hawse and I rode out from Louisiana with Mr. Gregory. Probably one of them mentioned my name."

"That must be it," Doc said, still puzzled. "Wait!" His eyes showed sudden interest and he asked, "You ain't no relationship to Marshal Fred Jury, are you?"

"I guess I am. He was my father."

"Was?"

"He was killed not long ago."

"I surely am sorry to hear that. I surely am. He was a good man. What happened?"

"He was shot down. Murdered," I said, having no better explanation.

"You figure someone came back for revenge? Someone he'd arrested and sent away to prison?"

I'd never even considered that. I had only just recently learned that my father had ever been a lawman. "I guess that could be, but then, he let these strangers stay on our farm. I don't suppose he'd do that if he knew them from his backtrail."

"No, I guess not. Maybe they out-talked him, made him believe they'd changed. Could be that they were friends of someone he'd sent up and he didn't know it when he invited them to stay."

"It could be. A lot of things could be, I guess. But he hadn't been a lawman for a long while, years and years."

"Prison terms can be long, Ben, and some people have long memories, real long."

"Well, it doesn't much matter why they did it. They're written down in my book now."

"You know who they are?" he asked with some surprise.

"Yes. I know."

I would say nothing more on the subject, and Doc didn't press it. He led me back into the kitchen, pulled out a wedge of cheese and some fresh bread which he sliced, making two thick sandwiches. He apologized for the meal.

"It's not much, but it'll hold you until morning. Then we'll have a proper breakfast—after I see if any of the other boys have trailed in for grub. After that I'll show you what needs to be done and where the tools are for the doing of it. I've been doing the yardwork myself, but it's interfering with my blacksmithing and farrier work, and at roundup time the boys lose shoes right and left, day and night."

"Is there anything you don't do around here, Doc?"

"Not much." His eyes were twinkling, and there was some pride in them as well. As if he was telling the world that he might be old, but he could still get the work done.

I was shown a bed at the end of the south bunkhouse and Doc gave me three blankets. "The nights have been cool." There was a small window over my bunk and one opposite through which I could see a few slowly traveling stars which I watched for a long thoughtful time until frost glazed over the window and sleep closed my eyes.

Come morning I rolled out with the chickens. I stood in the doorway of the bunkhouse drinking a cup of coffee made by Doc. Two cowboys had come in. Both had been riding night herd and were now dead to the world, rolled up in their blankets.

My first chore was cutting firewood. Grapevine used

plenty of it in its stoves and there always had to be a cord or so split and ready for the cooks. That work was not hard for me; I'd been cutting wood all of my life. Still, I had worked up a good sweat by eleven o'clock when Doc Parson caught up with me again. He eyed the pile of wood I had chopped and nodded with appreciation.

"That'll do for now. Looks like it will fill out the cook's cord. I've got something else for you to do," he said, handing me a folded piece of paper. "It's a list of supplies we need from town. I usually go myself. It's like a holiday for me. I get myself a beer and watch the ladies walk past. But"—he sighed—"I just got too much to do around here today."

"All right." I was happy to take a break from that woodpile.

"You can take the hay wagon . . . no, wait, darnit. It's got a wheel that needs greasing real bad. All right, then, take the buckboard. It's outside the barn, far side. Use the matched grays to pull it. They're fresh and could use the exercise."

"All right, Doc." I placed the folded list in my shirt pocket and buttoned it there. "Is there anything else I should know?"

"Well . . . can you read?"

"Yes."

"All right. Sometimes that darned Jack Turner at the store tries to short the boys who can't read what they're supposed to get. There is just one other thing—park the buckboard around back, in the alley, when you get to town. That's where the loading dock is, and the marshal, he don't like wagons parked out in the front street, cluttering it up."

"I understand." I put the axe away in the toolshed, went and got the gray horses from their stalls and hitched them to the buckboard and set out for La Paloma. Domino gave me a disappointed look as I drove the team past the corral he was sharing with six other horses.

The ride to town along the river road was pleasant, the sun warm, the glitter of the Brazos in the distance tranquil. Still, I kept a close eye on my backtrail, not knowing who might be following. With no problems at all I reached La Paloma, found the store and circled the block, using the alley as I drew up to the loading dock. Stepping inside, I gave my list to the helpful clerk and we went over it together briefly.

"How long will it take?"

"A little while. It's near lunch time now and I can't ask the boys to work through lunch. They get a little testy," he told me with a wink. He glanced at the clock on the wall. "Say an hour and a half to load you up. Is that all right?"

"Fine." I went out, using the front door this time. I stood beneath the awning, wiping out the sweat band of my hat, mopping my forehead with my bandanna.

"Hello, Ben Brown," a teasing voice said, and I turned to find Cora Brighton wearing a yellow dress and carrying a matching parasol. She wore a wide yellow and white hat with a lot of ribbons on it, cocked jauntily on her head.

"Hello, ma'am, how are you today?"

"I'm fine, thank you. I thought that you had moved on, but here you are again."

"Yes, ma'am. I took a job working out at Grapevine."

"I see," she said meditatively.

"Did Colin McCormick happen to return to town?"

"Well, yes," she said hesitantly. "Yes, he did, Ben."

"Did you give him my message?"

"Yes," Cora said quietly. "I did."

"Well? Did he say anything?"

"Well, Ben Brown, Colin said that he didn't really think you and he had anything to talk about."

"He did? I don't understand that. Where is he now, ma'am?"

"I don't think it is my place to tell you that," she said reservedly. We stood for a moment, looking at each other, saying nothing. Then she picked up her parasol, opened it and placed it over her shoulder. As she was stepping down into the street to cross toward the hotel, she smiled gaily back at me across her shoulder and said, "Ta-ta," before continuing on her way.

Well, that was that then! I guess I had no right to expect that McCormick would feel obliged to talk to me anyway. What was I to him? Trouble, if anything. Still, it kind of deflated me.

I had no appetite, and so instead of going to lunch I

just sat on the bench in front of the general store in the ribbon of shade cast by the awning and dozed for a while until the store clerk came out onto the boardwalk, shook my arm and told me, "Your order's ready."

I followed him inside, signed a form, a copy of which he gave me to take back to the ranch, and then after roughly checking the goods as Doc Parson had alerted me to do, I thanked the man, climbed onto the buckboard's seat and started the team of gray horses back toward Grapevine.

On the trail I began passing cowhands pushing small bunches of cattle southward. Reading the brands, I saw that these were men working for Lancaster, Gregory's neighbor, and other small ranches. It was roundup time and all of the ranches were scouring the range. Soon there would be very few range cattle around as they were gathered in a huge mixed herd, trail-branded and started toward a Kansas railhead.

I had to pull to the side of the road to let an arriving stagecoach pass. The stage driver waved a gloved hand in thanks as they raced past me, his six-horse team sweating heavily. I saw a pale face looking out at me from the uncomfortable confines of the coach, and then they were gone, leaving only a storm cloud of dust to mark their passing.

I decided to abandon the road to prevent another such occurrence, and guided the team of grays up and over a knoll strewn with wild oats. A few oak trees were scattered across the slope and there was a clump of trees near the crest. It was cool beneath the trees and as I was in no hurry, unlike the stage driver, I stopped for a while to let the gray horses blow and nibble at the sparse grass and the oats. Wrapping the reins around the brake handle, I stepped stiffly down.

I was not alone up there.

I heard a horse nicker and I automatically stepped nearer the shielding buckboard, resting my hand on my holstered Colt.

"Now what?" a sarcastic, familiar voice asked. "Are you planning to ambush me?"

I sighed and stepped out into the open again as Susan Gregory walked toward me, leading a leggy blue roan with a blaze on its nose.

"Hello, Miss Gregory."

"Hello," she returned, not sounding so angry as the night before. Walking to the rear of the buckboard, she began looking through the goods I had purchased in town.

"Did you bring a bolt of white lace?"

"It's in there somewhere. Turner's clerk wrapped it real careful, in brown paper."

She nodded, saying nothing else. She wore a pair of gray riding breeches, white blouse, and a yellow scarf around her throat. Hatless, her dark hair curled loosely over her shoulder. I wished she didn't dislike me.

"Would you mind if I rode along with you?" she asked, and she actually smiled, melting me.

"Not at all." My throat felt tight, my words a little

strangled. She just smiled again and I found my face glowing warm. I clambered aboard the buckboard and unwrapped the reins.

Before I realized what was happening, Susan was up beside me on the seat. "I thought . . ."

"Thought what? That I was going to ride that head-strong roan of mine when I can just sit up here and take it easy?" She looked at me thoughtfully. There was amusement in her eyes. "You *are* a funny man."

That rankled a little, but I said nothing in return. I was, after all, nothing but a hired hand, and she was the boss' daughter.

"Well! Let's get rolling, Ben." Her voice wasn't overly pleasant, but still it made me happy to have her there beside me. She had used my first name. Maybe there was hope yet that we might become friends. I sincerely hoped so.

I started the team on down the far slope, using the brake lightly to keep from running the buckboard up on the horses' heels.

The sunlight was pleasant through the foliage of the oaks, casting shifting shadows against the yellow grass. There were a few distant clouds, very white and high, and a crow sailing its low way across the sky. I could smell the cool scent of the Brazos River and the scent of the girl beside me. As we emerged from the trees I saw trouble coming. Fighting trouble.

Chapter Ten

"Get down!" I said roughly to Susan, astonishing her. "What? What are you talking about?"

I reined up sharply. "There's going to be trouble, Susan. Get down from the buckboard. Never mind. I'm borrowing your horse."

"You're not borrowing my . . . !" But already I was off the spring seat, tossing the reins to the grays to her. I stepped to the rear of the buckboard and untied Susan's tethered blue roan. I swung aboard, heeled the tall animal hard and pounded down the hillside, toward the lone rider I had seen there.

He was urging three Lancaster "Rafter L" cattle toward Lancaster's home ranch. He was still some distance off, his face only a smudge in the shadow of his wide-brimmed hat, but I recognized him even at that distance.

It was Brad, and I was going to collect what he owed me if I had to take it out of his hide.

He glanced my way, hearing the blue roan racing toward him. He didn't recognize the horse, nor know me at that distance. I saw him glance behind him and I let my gaze travel in that direction as well. I thought I knew who he was looking for. Scarface was never far away. The two men were never separated.

I did not see Scarface anywhere near, and it was open land I was riding across. Brad, still walking his horse, a coiled lariat in his right hand as he pushed the three yearling strays homeward, hadn't made a move yet.

Suddenly he stiffened in the saddle. I saw his mouth open and contort in a silent curse. By then it was already too late for him to attempt to elude me. I was riding Susan's blue roan flat out, and no matter what kind of starter Brad's mount was, it wasn't going to get up to speed quick enough to outrun me. I kicked my boots free of the stirrups and brought the roan directly beside Brad. I lunged from the saddle and hooked my arm around Brad's throat as I flew past him. We went over the side of his startled pony and hit the ground hard. The horses and cattle all scattered at the disturbance.

Brad came to his feet at the same time I did, looking murderous.

"You just won't let well enough alone, will you,

Jury!" he yelled, and he swung at my jaw with his right hand.

I managed to pull my chin back a couple of inches and his knuckles just grazed my face. As his fist swung past, I countered with my own right and, stepping in, followed with a left. Both blows connected, the right rocking Brad back on his heels, the following left banging against his windpipe.

Choking for breath, Brad swung at me again, but it was a feeble attempt. I dodged it and came in with an overhand right that caught him squarely on the nose. He went down to his knees, blood flowing freely from his nostrils. He tried to rise, strangling an angry curse, but I hit him again, with all the anger I had been holding back, a left that darted clean and sharp across the distance between us and split his cheek to the bone. Brad groaned and pitched forward on his face. He lay still, yet I hovered over him, both fists clenched, wishing he would rise and let me try it again.

"What are you doing? What is happening?" Susan was yelling. I hadn't heard the buckboard arrive—my entire focus had been on Brad. Now I turned to look at her, but I did not answer. On one knee, I rolled Brad over and turned his pocket inside out.

I found some of my money, about half of it. Scarface, of course would have the other half. I stood on shaky legs, wiping my hair back, panting from the brief battle.

"Are you crazy, Ben?" Susan wailed.

Again I did not answer her. Brad was coming around and I leaned over and yanked his Colt revolver from his holster, winging it away into the brush. I grabbed his shirtfront and yanked him to a sitting position.

"Where's your partner?" I demanded.

He only glared at me and then stupidly reached for his holster, finding it empty. "Go to hell, Jury," he said, shaking his head heavily. Streaks of blood, now caked with dust, led from his nostrils to his chin. His nose seemed to be swelling up. Good, I thought, I had broken it for him.

"Are you working for Lancaster, Brad? Or are you just licking up a few mavericks for yourself?"

"I ain't talking to you." He wiped the back of his hand across his bloody nose, winced in pain and growled at me. "We'll get you Jury. Next time we won't go so easy on you."

"What is all this about?" Susan demanded.

"Ain't you Gregory's daughter?" Brad asked, eyeing her darkly.

"Yes, I am," she said with a trace of haughtiness.

"Your daddy shouldn't let you go out ridin' with such men," Brad said with a sneer. Then he pulled a much-folded poster from his vest and tossed it toward Susan. It fluttered to the ground between her polished boots. "This here's what it's about, girl. He's an outlaw and he knows we're out to get him."

I saw Susan bend down and pick up the poster. Unfolding it she glanced at it and I saw her incredulous expression as she read those few words so familiar to me: *Wanted. Murder.*

"Susan," I said, snatching at the wanted poster, "it's nothing like you think."

She spun away, the poster still in her hand. Her eyes were heated, her lip trembling.

"That's right, Jury," Brad taunted. "Tell her how it is. Tell her that you're as innocent as a lamb and everyone else is wrong, even the law."

"Shut up!" I screamed, turning back toward him, my fists bunched. I wanted to beat him into the ground just then. I heard the creak of saddle leather behind me and then the sounds of a horse's hoofs being lifted into a run, and when I turned I saw Susan on her blue roan riding hard toward Grapevine, leaning low over the withers. Flagging her horse with her reins. Running away.

Escaping from me and my violence.

"Too bad," Brad said mockingly. His words didn't sting me. I found that I didn't care at that moment. I was already resigned to matters. There was no way to explain things to Susan. She wouldn't listen, and why should she? If she had disliked me before, now she must hate and fear me too.

"Get out of here, Brad," I said wearily. "You two just stay away from me, and we'll call it over. I won't come hunting you."

"You're wrong," Brad said, coming to his feet, rubbing his sore jaw. "It ain't over until we say it is."

He started walking toward his horse, but I sprinted to the animal, reaching it first. I drew my revolver as I held the shying horse. "Hold it right there, Brad."

"If you take my horse, I'll see you hung."

"Shut up, Brad. Just shut up!" I was tired of him, tired of everything.

I uncinched his saddle with one hand and threw it to the ground. Then I slapped the horse's rump hard and it took off again, running toward the river. I put a bullet into the air to keep it running.

"I wish you hadn't done that," Brad said.

I didn't answer. I walked back to the buckboard and climbed onto the seat, starting the matched grays back toward Grapevine, leaving Brad to shoulder his saddle and make the long walk back to Lancaster's spread.

Doc Parson was seated out in front of the bunkhouse, repairing a bit of harness, when I got back. I pulled the buckboard up, set the brake, and climbed down.

"Most of that stuff goes over to the big house," Doc told me.

"I know it. I'm sorry Doc, but I can't work here anymore."

"You can't . . ." He got to his feet, placing the harness aside. "Ben, you've only been here one day. What am I supposed to tell Mr. Gregory?"

"I don't think you'll have to tell him anything, Doc. He'll know by now that I'm leaving and why."

And that was that for my career as a ranch hand. I walked down to the corral and let Domino out.

Saddling up, I rode out of Grapevine as the sun lowered in the west, turning the face of the Brazos deep orange and velvet beyond the trees.

Where now? Where now, indeed, I asked myself angrily. I had gotten half of my money back from Brad, at least. I could find a less expensive place to sleep in La Paloma and try to contact McCormick again. He just might know something of Bouchonnet's and Twilly's whereabouts. He might even have a thought on how I could clear my name, maybe encourage Marshal Kent to arrest my father's killers.

Maybe.

McCormick had refused my last request to talk to me. And why was that? What had I done to him? Why wouldn't he see me? I didn't know but I meant to find out, because I continued to believe that he was the only person I knew who might be able to help me wriggle out of this mess. Until I did, I was just one more outlaw on the run, following the outlaw trail that led to nowhere but an early grave.

I figured that if McCormick was back in town, I could find him. La Paloma wasn't that large. Therefore, as I rode into town I angled Domino toward the largest, brightest saloon.

I walked through the bat wing doors with sunset at my back, and there he was. Colin McCormick sat at an octagonal card table, cigar between his fine teeth, dressed in a brushed gray suit and string tie.

He saw me all the way across the smoky room, looked again at his hand and then threw his cards down.

I saw him rise, say something to the other card players, scrape some gold coins from the table and stride toward me.

"Ben!" he said warmly, putting his hand out.

"Hello, Colin," I said, shaking his hand. I read nothing in his eyes. Not displeasure or apology. He was the same Colin McCormick I had known on the river.

"You've filled out some since I last saw you," he said. "And I could swear you've grown an inch or two taller." He put an arm around my shoulders as he turned me toward the door. "Where have you been, Ben?"

"Around," I said as we went out of the smoke-filled room and into the clear, cool evening. "Looking for you, mostly."

"Looking for me?" He laughed and spread his hands. "You see how easy I am to find!"

I hesitated, but told him, "I was told that you didn't want to see me, Colin." He stood peering into my eyes on the boardwalk. Two cowboys brushed by us and went into the saloon.

"Who told you that?" he asked, obviously surprised, perhaps upset, by my remark.

"I probably shouldn't say."

"Tell me." His words were an instruction to do as he asked, not a request.

"All right. It was Cora Brighton who relayed that

message to me. I understand you know her. Pretty well."

"That's right." He lit a thin cigar, cupping a match in his hand. The reddish flame illuminated a thoughtful expression. "You must have misunderstood what Cora told you, Ben. Or else she was kidding. Cora's a great kidder."

"That must be it," I agreed, not believing it for a second. I knew what Cora had told me, but not her reasons for it.

"La Paloma is the last place I expected us to meet again." McCormick flipped away his match and we watched its brief fiery descent.

"There are reasons I'm here, Colin." I looked around uncertainly. "This isn't really a good place to stand around discussing these things. Not for me."

"Oh?" He raised an inquiring eyebrow. "All right, then, how about coming up to my hotel room with me?"

"I don't want to interfere with your card game, Colin."

"It doesn't matter. The cards weren't running well tonight and those boys come to talk more than to lose money. Come along, we'll go up to my room and you can tell me what's happened to you since the riverboat."

That is what we did. In his room I started on my long story. It took me most of an hour to lay it all out, everything that happened and how matters now stood, me wanted for a hanging offense. I told him about the run-in with Brad and Scarface, with Doyle, the things I had been hearing and the little I had deduced.

"You have been busy, haven't you?" McCormick asked with a smile. He rose from his overstuffed chair and poured a bare inch of whiskey in a large glass.

"Yes, unfortunately. Still I haven't been able to locate Twilly and Bouchonnet, however; and that is my primary goal."

"Naturally." McCormick seated himself again, sipping at the amber liquid. "What about these other two men? What were their names?"

"As I tried to explain, they're the same two you met on board the *Sultan* when they tried to rob me. The heavy one with the dark whiskers is named Brad. I don't know his other name. The other I call Scarface because of that nasty scar across his mouth.

"Chiefly, Colin, they have just been a nuisance. It seems that they now feel that I have somehow done *them* an injury."

"That's the way thieves often think."

"They're just riffraff, not stone-cold killers like Bouchonnet and Mike Twilly."

"That doesn't mean they *wouldn't* shoot you, Ben. They might sit stewing one night until they determine to try it for the sake of the reward."

"I realize that, but they've had their chances. I think there must be something hanging over their heads as well. That they'd rather not get involved with the law."

"You could be right."

I was on my feet now, pacing in front of the balcony window. I stopped, hands behind my back. "I have to find a way to clear my name."

"Well, I know you didn't murder Wethers."

"I know you do, but even you can't claim to be an eye witness, Colin."

"No, I can't."

"I can't even prove that he was in your cabin, trying to rob you of your poker winnings."

"I know it, and that leaves us with a big problem, doesn't it?" He finished his drink and placed the glass on the small round table holding the lantern. Its smoky light illuminated the room, flickering and shifting across their faces. "Ironically Brad and this Scarface *were* actual eye witnesses. At least, they were there in the ship's passageway."

"They would never admit that," I said dismally.

"No."

"And so, in the eyes of the law I am a murderer and will remain one. I'm fair game for any man with a gun. And I have to have that hanging over my head while I'm trying to hunt down my father's killers. It's a damnable mess, Colin."

"I haven't seen that gang, anyone who resembles Bouchonnet or Twilly, in La Paloma. Nor have I heard a word. I can start asking around, however."

"It's a mess, a real mess," I repeated, feeling sorry for myself.

McCormick got up and stretched. Looking at me, he changed the subject and asked, "Could you stand to make some money, Ben? Some good money for very little work?"

"Of course I could," I said eagerly, but I grew wary. "What sort of work did you have in mind?"

"You might not want to get involved after I've told you, but in any case, I have to have your promise that you won't reveal this scheme of mine to anyone."

"Of course I wouldn't." I narrowed my eyes, wondering about this man and his secret ways once again.

"We're going to try to get ourselves involved in a stagecoach holdup." There was no smile on McCormick's lips. He was dead serious.

"You!" I said in disbelief. "Were you the lone gunman who stuck up that stage, Colin?" I knew he had been out of town. I knew that Cora had lied about his whereabouts. I knew . . . what did I know? "That road agent was you, Colin?"

He stared at me for a long moment and then burst out laughing, shaking his head. "Ben, Ben, of course that wasn't me. Do you take me for a stickup man? You do seem to get your ideas all tangled. When I said we are going to try to get ourselves involved in one, I meant on the other side. We're trying to prevent another stickup. It's a trap for the robber we have in mind."

"A trap?" I felt a little numb and quite silly. I should have had more confidence in McCormick, in the man I believed him to be.

"Certainly. We've got to stop these stage robberies. It's getting to where no one can count on anything coming in or going out of La Paloma safely—cash, contracts, business letters, deeds . . . no, we've got to stop this."

"Marshal Kent . . ."

"Alvin Kent is a decent, honest man. He is, however, not up to this. He hasn't got the skills for it. He hasn't the nerve. He's a good enough town marshal all right. He locks up drunks at night, collects his fines, but that's about it. A lot of people are unhappy with this, especially the stage line. I have agreed to work for them on stopping the robberies. For a price," he added.

"A good price, I take it."

"The amount needn't concern you, Ben, but I can use some help. From someone I can trust."

"Would they want me in on this? Someone might know that I'm a wanted man."

"No one but me will need to know you're working with me."

"Just who are the others, Colin? If this is to trap the robbers, it must be a closely held secret. Men who can be trusted without reservations."

"Exactly. Only three people know. The manager of the Colton-Western stage line, George Potter; the banker, Howard Tanner, and me."

"Not the marshal?" I asked with surprise.

"No. He's not involved in the operation. It's not strictly a town matter; he doesn't need to know."

"What is it that you want me to do?" I had accepted the idea that I would work with McCormick and perhaps in the process burnish my blackened reputation with influential people.

"You will be riding inside the coach, Ben. You'll have a shotgun. Ben," he asked me with some concern, "do you think you will be all right with this? What I mean, is if it came down to it, could you shoot a robber?"

I took in a long slow breath and nodded. "I could, Colin. Now. If it came down to having to do it, I could. *Only* if there is no other way, though."

"Good." McCormick's relief was patent. "That is the kind of answer I wanted. I don't want a gun-happy yahoo along. There may be more than one of them, Ben. I imagine that there was more than one the last time. It's just that only one of the robbers showed himself on the trail. I would wager there was a second man, maybe a third and a fourth, watching from cover. That's the way I would do it. There may be a lot of shooting, Ben."

"I understand."

"All right, then. It's tomorrow. The stage leaves at seven-fifteen. We'll be loading a strongbox for everyone to see, but it will be empty. We make the run and hope the robbers hit us. If not, we'll try running the decoy again and again until they do try it. If you don't recognize me, I'll be driving the stage."

"If I don't recognize you?"

I had to smile as he went to his closet and pulled out

an old greasy pair of jeans, a faded red shirt with a hole at the elbow and a torn flop hat. "The new me," he said.

Putting the old clothes away, he said, "You get into the coach while it's still in the shed getting the team hitched. Lean back, stay low. Keep the side curtains down. Try not to let anyone see you. Not a soul, just in case the highwaymen are watching."

"All right. I can do that."

"Right," he said with satisfaction. Reaching into the closet again he withdrew a double-twelve scattergun and a box of shells loaded with buckshot, handing them to me.

"Ben, are you sure you want to do this? It could get very dangerous."

"I'm sure, I answered." Surprisingly, I *was* sure. I felt calm and capable of doing my part even though I knew how dangerous it could become. I don't know what it was, maybe the nearness of McCormick and his own aura of confidence, but I felt man enough to face the stagecoach robbers if they did come.

"I've got to be getting along, Colin," I said, hefting the shotgun. "I have to find myself a room for the night."

"You're staying in the hotel, Ben. Ask for your old room back. I'm paying—or rather the company is." I had started toward the door. Now I halted and very slowly turned back. "My old room?"

"Yes."

"Colin—you told me that you hadn't even known I

was in La Paloma. Now you you're saying that you not only knew, but knew that I was staying in this very hotel."

He hesitated only fractionally. "I just found out today. Cora admitted it."

"You said she hadn't."

"I didn't want you to be angry with her, Ben. She has her funny ways, you know."

"No, I don't." I supposed it made no real difference now, still I continued to have to fence with the truth and I didn't like it. No one seemed to want to be totally honest with me, and I couldn't understand it. I had only one more question to ask before I left the room.

"How well did you know Fred Jury, Colin?"

His face went bloodless white and his eyes narrowed fiercely for just a moment, and when he finally answered, smiling, I knew that he was not going to tell me the truth about my dead father.

Still I listened.

Chapter Eleven

Colin McCormick and I stood facing each other in his hotel room. The night breeze shifted the white curtains over the open window and we could hear men shouting from a nearby saloon. It was a long time before he answered my question.

"How well did you know Fred Jury, Colin?"

"He was your father, then?"

"I think you already knew that." I couldn't understand his reluctance to give me a direct answer. I waited.

"I didn't know that. I might have guessed," he said with a slight shrug of his broad shoulders. "How well did I know him?" He looked past me for a minute and then his eyes met mine again. His smile was even. "It's been quite a while since he was marshal here, Ben. Years and years."

164

"I know." He was still being evasive. I continued to wait for an honest answer.

"I guess you would say that I knew him as well as any other town marshal we've had since his time. No better, no less."

"Is that the whole truth, Colin?"

"Of course it is! Why? Is there some reason you persist in asking me these questions?"

"No," I said tiredly. There was, of course, but I could see I wasn't going to get any straight answers to my questions anyway. I just had the gnawing feeling that there was something buried in the past that concerned me and no one wanted to reveal. But then again, I told myself, maybe it was something that should remain buried.

"How do I go about getting a key to my room?" I asked, abandoning the pointless conversation.

"I'll go down to the desk with you," McCormick said, apparently relieved at my change in attitude. "I have to be going out again anyway."

He rested his hand on my shoulder as we walked along the hallway toward the stairs. Neither of us spoke. There was nothing to talk about just then. The past was a mystery; tomorrow was a secret we must not be heard speaking of.

We paused at the desk, McCormick obtaining my key without—I noticed as I signed the register—any money passing between him and the room clerk.

"I'll be seeing you, Ben," McCormick said. Just for a

moment he hesitated, looking at me as I stood there, double-barreled shotgun in my hand, but he said nothing, touched his hat brim and turned to stride out of the hotel.

I returned to the room I had previously occupied, but I did not go out onto the balcony. I just lay on the bed, fully clothed and stared at the ceiling, thinking circular thoughts. Unable to sleep a wink, I rose, went back out and delivered Domino to the stable.

On the way back I stopped in a restaurant for a cup of coffee and a slice of apple pie, and then returned to the room to lock the door and sleep soundly until sunlight began streaming through the sheer curtains.

It was very quiet on the main streets of La Paloma as I looked out the window, pulling my belt tight. Long shadows from across the street lay at the feet of the false-fronted buildings along my way as I walked the rutted street, shotgun in my hand, my holster tied down.

I saw a cowboy sleeping it off in an alley, a kid with a fishing pole, spotted white pup at his heels, and the minister rushing toward his white, steepled church. An old man was sweeping out the hardware store, but he didn't even look up as I went by. No one else appeared across all of the town until I reached the barn where the stagecoaches were kept.

"Hold it right there!" a voice from the shadowed corner of the barn commanded. "I got my sights on you."

"Take it easy. I'm supposed to be here."

"Yeah? Who are you?"

"Ben Brown," I said, not knowing which name McCormick gave them. "I'm riding with Colin McCormick."

"All right, then," the man said, and a figure emerged from behind a stack of hay bales. Small, worried-looking, extremely wrinkled, he didn't bother to introduce himself.

"We won't be hitching up for a good hour yet," he said.

"Yeah, I know. I just wanted to come on over before half the town was awake to watch me walking down the street with this greener in my hand."

"Good idea," the man said, eyeing the shotgun. "Look, Brown, if you're going to hang around and watch, I could use a cup of coffee across the street."

"Go ahead," I said.

"Appreciate it."

I sat on the hay bales, shotgun on my lap, watching the shadows slowly shift as the morning passed. After twenty minutes or so, the guard came back, nodding his thanks. We waited together, not speaking, until two men arrived at just about seven, leading a team of horses.

"Hello, Ed!" one of them called to my silent friend. "I'm surprised to see you around this early. What's up?" His eyes shifted from Ed to me and back again.

"Nothin'. The boss just thought that someone's been fooling around the stables when no one's here. Maybe some drunks using our hay for a cot. He asked me to watch overnight. This here's Mr. Brown," he said, nodding at me. "He's riding along in the coach."

"Yeah? So?"

"So it's just that . . . you didn't see Mr. Brown, Carl, get me?"

Carl shrugged. "Whatever you say. It all pays the same. He can do what he wants as far as I'm concerned."

I did just that, clambering into the coach, lowering the dust curtains while the men hitched the team to the stage. Then I waited silently, listening to the chink of trace chains, the shifting of the horses' impatient hoofs, the muted curses of the hostlers.

At seven-fifteen the stagecoach was pulled out of the barn and the team led to the stage depot to await the driver. I peered out through a curtain gap, but could not see McCormick yet. The excitable stage stop manager was there arguing with Ed, the stable guard. A few suitcases sat on the plankwalk. I frowned deeply. Someone would be riding with me, it seemed. That was not part of the plan, and I was pretty sure that was what the discussion was about. Waving his hands in frustration, the manager went back into his office. How he was going to explain that this particular stage was taking no passengers, I could only guess.

A minute later I spotted McCormick. Slouched, wearing the old clothes he had shown me the night before, unshaven, he walked to the coach, helping Ed carry the iron strongbox which they loaded with apparent difficulty, even though I knew it was empty.

I let the side curtain fall back in place, and sat there in the dry, warm silence waiting to begin.

The stagecoach door was suddenly flung open and I flinched, gripping my shotgun tighter. The sunlight behind her was blindingly brilliant, but I knew her anyway.

"Susan!"

"Hello, Ben," Susan Gregory answered coolly, and Ed gave her a hand aboard as she climbed into the stage holding her dark green velvet skirts up.

She sat opposite me, smiling. She was no longer angry, so far as I could tell, but . . .

"What are you doing on this stage?" I asked anxiously.

"Going to Kansas. Father's driving the big herd up next week, I'm going ahead to meet him there."

"But you can't—"

"Take this particular coach? Of course I can." Her voice had the ring of authority. Her family, of course, was privileged in these parts. She would do as she liked. "Why does everyone keep telling me that I cannot leave when I choose? I have purchased a ticket, and I may certainly go when I wish. I'll not take all of my trunks back to Grapevine and come back when it suits everyone else."

And that settled that, it seemed.

I studied her as McCormick cracked the whip over the horses' ears and the coach lurched into motion. Susan had rolled up one of the dust curtains and by the light I could see her very clearly, and I read no sign of surprise or annoyance at riding with me.

"What's happened? I thought you hated me," I said.

"Oh, that!" She waved a hand. "That didn't mean anything. I do have a temper if you haven't noticed."

"Of course, but—"

"I talked to my father. He explained things to me."

"And you believed him?"

"He's my father," she said with conviction.

"Yes, but Susan, he wasn't there either when the trouble began."

"No. Colin McCormick was, though."

"You talked to Colin about it?"

"Only this morning when he took me aside and tried to talk me out of coming along on this trip."

"What did he say?"

"That you were trustworthy and truthful and generally a fine young man," she answered, her eyes meeting mine directly.

"Didn't he tell you how wrong you were to take this coach?"

"Yes. He didn't say why, of course, but it isn't hard to figure out if you've got half a brain. You expect a robbery attempt to be made on the stage, don't you?"

"Yes, since you seem to know already."

"I figured that out immediately. But listen, Ben, why should that stop me? There's always the danger that any stage will be held up out here—any day of the week. There's a risk that the Kiowas might decide to raid one.

Ben, I am a Western woman. I accept these risks. If one doesn't, she might as well hide her head under the blankets and never come out."

"People were just trying to look out for you, Susan."

"I understand. I really do." She looked out the window, watching the land drift past. We had cleared town and were now in open country, following the river road. She scooted forward on her seat and bent toward me a bit.

"Ben, we're going to be together on this coach for a long time. Why don't you just begin at the beginning and tell me your life story?"

And I did, cutting a few corners here and there, omitting a few things, but as the miles ran past, I found myself opening up as I could not remember having done with anyone else. And it seemed that Susan really was interested in me. I found that I wanted her to know everything about me, and it seemed she wanted to learn.

"Well," she said at one point in my narrative, "it doesn't seem that things have been too easy for you since leaving home. I'm sorry we got off on the wrong foot in town. I was hot and tired that day. And," she laughed, "I'm a brat!"

It was just then that the first shot rang out.

I reached for the window, but the coach suddenly swerved violently. My first thought was they'd shot McCormick because the coach swung wide to the right and then severely back to the left. As they jumped from the ruts, the left side wheels were wrenched away savagely and the coach rolled.

Susan was on top of me and then I on top of her. Dust stormed through the interior of the coach. We lay tangled in confusion.

I raised up first, reached out and slammed the coach door open. I looked up to see two men riding down on us, approaching fast. I cut loose with the shotgun, giving them both barrels of double-ought buckshot. I don't know if I hit either of them, but they swerved away at a dead gallop, riding right past the downed coach.

I could see that the entire team had come free of the coach. One lay still in its harness, its neck obviously broken from a tumbling roll.

"Ben!" Susan cried out.

"Come on," I encouraged her, "we've got to get out of here."

I reached down, gripped her wrist and towed her up beside me. I helped her clamber up onto the side of the coach. She let go and slid to the ground past the still-spinning rear wheel. I followed her. As I hit the ground three or four shots sprayed the coachwork of the wrecked stage. I fired back blindly with my Colt, aiming at the puffs of smoke rising from behind the willow brush along the river.

"Come on!" I shouted and, taking Susan's hand, I pulled her after me as we raced for the cover of the brush and scattered boulders up the hillside behind us.

We dove behind reddish boulders as someone with a rifle threw two quick shots our way. The bullets ricocheted off the granite.

Then it was silent. No one moved. There was no sound but the wind rustling in the trees. The river flowed past moodily. Susan touched my arm.

"Do you think they've gone?"

"Not a chance. They want the strongbox. It's empty, but they don't know that. They're trying to figure out a way to eliminate us."

"We could just slip away."

"I'd almost be willing, if I thought they'd let us. But what about Colin?"

"Where is he?" she asked, worriedly studying the road, the overturned coach below us.

"I don't know, but he might be down there, badly hurt, needing help."

"How long will they wait before they try something?"

"They won't put it off too long, someone might come up the road. A posse for all they know. They'll have to make a try for the strongbox soon."

"Maybe they'll just give it up, maybe they will," Susan said, but it was only wishful thinking and we both knew it.

Where was Colin?

I was worried about McCormick, deeply worried, but my biggest concern was not for him, but for Susan. If McCormick was still alive down there, he was able to defend himself. Susan—that was another story. I was torn between trying to elude the robbers and standing by my friend.

"Of all days to wear my best dress," Susan complained. I couldn't help it: I laughed, and so did she, releasing some of our tension.

"Look, Susan. We've got to put some more distance between us and them. Withdraw farther up the hill."

"All right," she said.

I surveyed the land behind us. The ground was fairly well covered by sumac, purple sage and scrub oak. It was low brush, but I thought we could make our way upslope to relative safety. It would leave the outlaws a lot of ground to cover if they tried to rush us. I was leaving myself almost no chance of doing the job I had been hired to do—capturing the robbers—but Susan's safety came first. I also felt as if I was running away from McCormick in his time of need, but this was the only move that made sense to me.

"We'll give it a try. Are you ready?" I asked and Susan nodded bravely, gathering up her skirts.

Running in a crouch then, with Susan leading the way, me with my Colt following, we zigzagged our way up the slope. Branches scraped my face and snagged my shirt. Susan had even rougher going, the way she was dressed, but I didn't hear her mutter a word of complaint. She was a strong lady, this one, and I found myself admiring her for it.

I became aware of oncoming sounds and I looked back through the screen of brush, watching as three horsemen rushed toward the downed stagecoach. Let them have it. There was nothing worth a cent down there. The day had been a tragedy, a useless violent time for all involved.

We struggled to the crest of the hill and Susan, unable to go on, sank heavily to the ground. When a man raised up from the brush behind her, I shot without thinking.

He had triggered off first and his bullet blasted past me so near that I heard a rush of wind as it passed my ear. The answering shot from my .44 Colt slammed into his body just below the heart. He threw his hands wildly into the air, his eyes rolled back and the masked bandit crumpled to the ground.

Below us, near the stage, I saw the other raiders pause and look our way, but they made no move to come toward us. They were busy trying to pry open the empty strongbox.

Susan was trembling. The badman had fallen not five feet from her. I raised Susan gently and hugged her for a long minute, hiding my own shaking. My eyes were still on the men below as they rifled the stage and continued working on the strongbox. I heard distant cursing, grumbling. They had gotten the box open and now I saw one of them kick it angrily. It rung with a hollow resonance.

After a few more moments of savage cursing and exchanged recriminations, the raiders remounted their horses and rode off in a file toward the Brazos.

"Are you all right?" I asked Susan. My finger wiped a tear from her cheek. She nodded mutely, biting at her lower lip.

"Go ahead a little way, will you, Susan?" I asked, helping her to her feet. I wanted to look at the dead man's face. Maybe seeing it would give me a clue as to who the raiders were.

Susan nodded and walked slowly on, her back proud and straight, her new green velvet dress studded with burrs and dead grass. I went to the dead man and rolled him over. Then I tugged his bandanna mask down.

It was Marshal Alvin Kent.

"Holy . . . !" I exclaimed, going to my knees while staring at the man I had killed.

Susan heard me and turned back anxiously. I was still on my knees gawking when she stood over me, her shadow falling across the dead marshal's face.

"No wonder," Susan said. "No wonder he could never catch any of the highwaymen."

"No wonder Colin wouldn't share our plan with him."

"Colin!" we both said nearly at once. The outlaws were gone. We could make our way back down to the overturned stagecoach and the team, anchored by the dead horse.

Once we were down the long brushy slope again, I told Susan, "Wait here, all right?" I reloaded the shot-gun and gave it to her. She handled it expertly. As she herself had said, she was a Western woman. Guns were nothing new to her.

"What are you going to do, Ben?"

"Colin must have been thrown from the box back a way. Where we first felt the horses stumble and the coach go loose under us. I mean to have a look."

"Then why . . . ?" she asked, touching my sleeve, looking up into my eyes.

"It's best if you just wait here," I said firmly. I was going to try to find McCormick. If the worst had happened, I did not want her to see another dead man on that morning. I feared the worst because it had been nearly an hour since the onset of the attack, and McCormick had not called out, nor had he fired a shot during the brief battle.

Quail rustled in the underbrush. The river muscled its way past, rolling southward toward the gulf. Clouds of white cotton spun past overhead. The sky was pale and the air along the river warm, humid and alive with insects. I found McCormick a quarter of a mile back from the wrecked stage.

"Ben, what took you so long?"

I grinned until my lips hurt. He was sitting on the river side of the road, blood drenching one pantleg, his face bruised and scratched, but he was smiling at me!

"I dunno. Lazy, I guess. We figured you could make out on your own, anyway; you always have."

"I have. But right now, old son . . . I could use just a little help."

I slit his pantleg open and was stunned to find his leg barely damaged. It had bled like crazy, but the flow had stemmed to a trickle. Miraculously, only muscle, not bone had been tagged by the spinning lead. I bound his leg as tightly as I could and McCormick, with his eyes slightly glazed, asked me, "How's it look, Ben?"

"I'd say you don't have long. Maybe forty, fifty years."

McCormick smiled again. He was weak and wobbly when I got him to his feet, but we managed to make our way back to Susan.

She had managed to get the team hitched!

She had cut the dead horse from the harness and backed the other three into their traces. The coach was upright. It had come to its wheels as she led the team forward across the ruts. She had told me that she was a woman of the West. Now I was starting to understand just how much woman she was.

"Is he all right?" Susan asked worriedly as we reached her.

"Just ask me, girl," McCormick said with a weak growl. "There's still enough left of me to talk."

Susan smiled and touched his cheek with the back of her hand. She leaned down and closed the lid on the empty strongbox, shaking her head. "The things men are willing to kill each other over," she commented quietly. "I wonder what they thought when they opened it?"

"You wouldn't want to know," McCormick guessed.

"Colin," I said, "I had to kill one of them."

"You did? Was it anyone you recognized?"

"Yes, you could say that."

Susan blurted it out. "It was Marshal Kent!"

"Kent!"

"Yes, Colin. Where does that leave me now?" I thought of the posters out on me already: Murderer, horse thief. Now I had killed a lawman.

"How did it happen?" he asked, his expression dark.

"He tried to shoot me."

"I was there," Susan said. "A Gregory's word counts for something in this county."

"So does mine, I hope," McCormick said. "Did you manage to get a look at the others?"

"They were masked. We were too far away."

"I see." His expression shifted to resignation. "Listen, you two, it was *me* who shot Marshal Kent, do you understand?"

"I can't let you, Colin," I objected.

"It was me that did it," he repeated roughly. "You need no more trouble just now, Ben."

Reluctantly I agreed. I knew that he was right.

"We'll send a wagon back for his body. For now," he said, slurring his words a little as he leaned heavily against the stagecoach, "I'm afraid I'm getting a little dizzy and must sit down."

"What you must do is get back to town to the doctor," Susan said, taking charge.

We helped McCormick into the bullet-riddled stagecoach and watched him lean his head back wearily, closing his eyes. His leg was beginning to bleed profusely again, but La Paloma was not that far away, and there was a doctor of good reputation in the town. He had seen more than his share of bullet wounds. McCormick would be in good hands.

I climbed up into the box and took the reins. Then, sitting very near Susan, I started to turn the team back toward La Paloma. My thoughts just then were not on my driving or even on the holdup. I found myself thinking how pretty Susan looked even with her hair unpinned, her clothes filled with stickers, and her nose smudged with dust.

I took it as easy as possible on the way in. I said little to Susan, but I was thinking deeply. Thinking dark and angry thoughts. I saw her watching my scowling face and I suppose she could stand my dark silence no longer, because she said sternly: "It's over, Ben. Colin will be all right."

"Yes, Colin will be all right." Unless, I sullenly reflected, something went wrong, gangrene maybe setting in, and the doctor had to remove his leg. "But, this is far from over, Susan."

The stagecoach hit a large rock due to my inattention and jolted us roughly. I apologized mentally to McCormick.

"What do you mean when you say that it's not over, Ben?" Susan asked. Her eyes were filled with concern. "Marshal Kent was behind the gang. He's dead now."

"He was the leader, yes, but don't you understand who the rest of the gang is? Men who were recruited from all over to share in the wealth. Four of them I feel fairly certain I have known personally. One of these shot Colin . . . and, Susan, two of them are the men who killed my father. Susan, I know who they are."

"You mean those men you were following?"

"Of course. Why else would they have come all the way to Texas, to a punk town like La Paloma? To make some quick money holding up the stagecoaches. It was Bouchonnet and Twilly. There's no doubt in my mind. And probably Brad and Scarface. Those two have no reason to be here either except mercenary ones. I'm positive they are the gang members. I'm going to get them, Susan, I swear it."

"You don't have to! This has nothing to do with you anymore."

"It has everything to do with me, Susan," I said quietly and she fell into subdued silence.

We were within sight of the town, and I called down to see if McCormick was all right. His answer was only a feeble murmur, and I hurried the team on.

I drew up in a swirl of dust before the doctor's office. The townspeople had seen me coming from a mile away and knew that something was wrong. A crowd gathered immediately as I hopped from the box of the rocking coach, assisting Susan to the ground. Through the crowd I saw Cora Brighton fighting her way forward, her hair half-pinned up, her eyes wide.

"Who is it? Who's hurt?" I heard her demanding. Then she burst from the crowd and I found myself facing the anguished woman.

"It's Colin," I had to tell her. "I don't think it's real bad, but he's lost a lot of blood. Someone help me get him into the doctor's office!"

"Get out of my way!" Cora said sharply. Her mouth was set, her eyes determined. She stepped up into the coach and helped me lift him out as gently as we could. She too, I decided then, was a lot of woman. We got McCormick inside and laid him on the cot in the doctor's office, and the medical man began buzzing around, cutting away his pantleg and my rough bandage.

He shooed us away. "Go on! There's nothing any of you can do to help."

We went out and stood in a ragged group on the plankwalk in the shade of the office awning. The hostlers from the stage line had come up and retrieved the team. The streets had emptied of curiosity-seekers already. It was only of small interest in this frontier town that McCormick had been shot. Men were shot daily in La Paloma.

"What are you going to do now, Ben?" Cora asked me, brushing a tendril of her reddish hair from her eyes. The dry wind twisted down the street, nudging a tumbleweed along. I took a long time answering.

"I'm going after those killers, ma'am."

"You can't do that alone! Wait for help. The county sheriff, maybe."

"I can't wait. They may decide to blow out of the area by then. I'm going hunting for them."

Susan was looking up at me unhappily, but she spoke to Cora.

"Don't waste your breath talking to him, Miss Cora. If Ben says he's going, well, he'll go. I know him that well already."

Susan was right, of course. I hadn't come this far to quit now. Cora said nothing else, but studied me with concern as I took a deep breath and turned toward the stable. Susan said nothing either, but she touched my elbow to halt me and when I turned she got to tiptoes and kissed my cheek once before I turned again and started walking to where I had left Domino.

It was time to begin the hunting again, and this time I carried in my heart no compunctions about shooting down the outlaw raiders. None at all.

Chapter Twelve

I saw Domino's black and white head lift in the stall as I entered the dark and musty stable, and I had to grin. Then the shadowy figure of a man moved out of the shadows beside me and my hand flashed down to the butt of my Colt.

"Easy, friend," a familiar voice said, and I saw the toothless grin of Randall Hawse.

"What are you doing here?"

"I come to help," Randall answered flatly. "That is, if you can use some help."

"Sure I can. But what about Gregory? The trail drive?"

"I'll catch up with them when I can. If I can. If not"—he shrugged—"well I ain't so sure anymore that

I've got the makings of a cowboy. I'll find something else to do."

"There'll be shooting along this trail, Randall," I warned him soberly.

"I figured as much, Ben."

"I wouldn't want to see you hurt."

"I wouldn't want to see you hurt either, old friend. That's why I'm wishing to go with you if you'll have me." I studied the sincerity in his eyes for a long moment then nodded my thanks.

We said nothing else. I saddled Domino and we rode our horses out of town at a walk. Passing the doctor's window I saw Susan looking out from behind the corner of a curtain, but I did not turn my head or wave. It was hard enough to be riding away from her as it was.

We rode back to the scene of the stage holdup and searched the area carefully. There was a confusion of tracks in all directions, the road being well-traveled as it was, but eventually we came across a place where three horses had come together and lined out at a gallop toward the Brazos River. Only three horses. I had expected to find four, but then I had warned Brad off earlier after our fight; maybe he had taken my advice and cleared out.

"That looks like blood there," Randall pointed out as we passed a huge clump of glossy sumac. I nodded. I had seen crimson spots on the sandy ground a little way back. One of them had been hit during the fight, most likely one of the two who had charged my shotgun.

Randall and I rode on into the sun. The river passed us, gleaming in sunlight, deeply mottled in the shade of the riverside trees. On the banks of the river we came up on a place where the bandits had gotten down and allowed their horses to drink. There were larger spots of blood on the sandy earth.

"Whoever he is, he's hit pretty bad," Randall said.

"No telling who it was. I'd like to know, though it makes no difference."

"We'll catch up with him anyway," Randall said grimly. "These men aren't the sort to slow down on account of a wounded partner."

He was right, of course, which made me wonder if their plan might be to simply leave the wounded man behind to snipe at us and so possibly be rid of him and us with one stroke. I started keeping a closer watch on possible hiding places in the willows along the river. For now, however, the three horses tracked straight ahead, riding northward along the riverbank, taking no pains to hide their tracks. Perhaps they believed no posse could be raised in a short enough time to have a chance at catching up.

"Do you have any idea where they might be heading, Ben?" Randall asked.

"No, I have no better idea than you do."

Which was another large advantage the killers had. They knew the area and their destination, probably determined well in advance of the holdup attempt.

"What's that?" Randall asked. We had followed their

tracks leading up from the sandy river bottom toward a small, bare knoll beyond. Cresting out we found ourselves looking down into a wedge-shaped valley where dry buffalo grass and scattered sage grew. Farther along there was a stand of cottonwood trees, their leaves turning brightly in the high sun, showing silver on their underside. And beyond them we could see a tendril of lazily rising smoke, a thread of gray against the bright blue of sky.

"A cabin?" Randall suggested.

"I don't know. It could be anything. Anyone at all."

"If the outlaws don't know we're trailing them, Ben, it could be that we've got a chance to take them while they're napping."

"It could be," I answered, but I doubted it. Men on the run from the noose aren't apt to get that careless. There would surely be somebody watching the back-trail if it was the men we were pursuing. "Let's circle wide," I said. "We'll try coming up on the smoke from the north. There's a lot of trees bunched up on that side of the camp, and they won't be expecting pursuit from that direction."

"It could be just a hunter, Ben. Kiowas, maybe. It'll cost us a lot of time if we're wrong." His eyes were narrow as we sat our horses on the dry knoll. The sun beat down on our shoulders, hotter now than ever.

"I know it, Randall," I said grimly. But I wasn't wrong. I don't know why I was so sure, but I knew the outlaw gang was there in that copse. Maybe they had decided that their horses needed rest if they were planning to make a long run of it. Maybe they had left fresh mounts hidden there waiting for them. Maybe they had taken pity on the wounded man after all and decided to stop and doctor him up. I didn't know their motives, but I *knew* they were there. I felt it like you can feel a thunderstorm building up without really knowing how you know it.

"Let's try it, Randall. Quickly, but keep to all the cover we can find."

We turned our backs to the river and began making our way eastward through the oak and pinyon pine trees, and then gradually north. We could still see the smoke. It did not rise high, for the wind whipped it away. Now and then, we caught a glimpse of a squat, weathered cabin. One of their horses nickered. It was a far away sound, but Domino heard it, and his ears pricked up.

The day continued hot and silent except for the horses' hoofs crunching dry grass and gravel underfoot. Sweat trickled down the back of my neck and stained my shirtfront. It must have taken us an hour to get to the cottonwood sheltered hillside to the north, and we reined in there, studying the cabin.

"They're still there," Randall said. His face betrayed his nervousness now. I imagine mine mirrored his own. If you're not afraid to ride into another man's gunsights, you have to be a fool or plain crazy.

"I wish I knew if all of them are inside," I said in a low voice.

But there was no way of knowing that. We sat on that knoll for a long time, the horses shifting restlessly. I don't know what thoughts were running through Randall's mind. For myself I was just wishing that everything could have been different, that I was back home on our little farm with Pa.

Wishing doesn't change a thing.

"Come on," I said more roughly than I intended. We checked the loads in our pistols and started down. We were committed to a course of action now, and there was no more point in reluctance. Or even in caution.

We rode with our spurs flashing now, though I seldom touched Domino's flanks with them, and he knew there was something different about this ride, something urgent within me. We crossed the little valley swiftly, the horses' hoofs fairly singing though the grass as the wind bent back the brims of our hats and cooled the sweat on our chests and faces.

The rifle rang out when we were within a hundred yards of the cabin. I saw the puff of smoke first and a split second later heard the cracking report of a Winchester. I don't know how close that shot came nor the two that rapidly followed. We just rode on at breakneck speed, low across the withers of the galloping horses, our guns in hand. I didn't even remember drawing my revolver, nor had I fired it yet, though

Randall had winged a random shot at the sniper in the trees.

We approached the cabin at a full gallop and the hundred yards we had to cross was eaten up in no time by Domino's flying legs.

Reaching the windowless back wall of the cabin, I slowed Domino and swung to the side of the saddle, dropping from the horse, careening to a stop against the gray plank wall as Domino ran on. Randall tried the same maneuver, took a tumble and was a moment collecting his wind to rise. I was waving frantically to him. I saw the rifleman's next shot pick up a puff of dust a few feet from Randall's head. That got him moving. He stumbled to where I waited, pistol held high, barrel beside my ear.

The rifleman no longer had the angle to see us or do any damage. But the two men in the house had certainly been alerted by the gunfire, and so far as I knew the only approaches were the front door and the front window covered with oiled paper, as was usual in these parts.

"Think there's another window?" I asked.

"I couldn't get a look at the other side. Want me to take a peek?"

"That's the rifleman's side."

"Hell, he's proven to me that he can't shoot," Randall said with a grin, and before I could reply, he moved off in a crouch toward the far corner. I saw him peer around the corner without drawing a shot, and then he edged back toward me, nodding.

"It's high up, but there's one there."

"Big enough to get through?"

"Yes, but—"

I interrupted Randall, This was no time for debate. "I'll try to draw them both to the front of the house. If you can get to that window when the shooting starts . . ."

"They might be watching it, Ben!"

"Want to trade jobs?"

"No," he said with a shake of his head. "All right, Ben." He took a deep breath, let it out slowly and then grinned toothlessly. "Good luck."

"Hell, Randall, there's only three of them," I said with false bravado. But we were going to need luck and more than a little of it. We had two outlaws forted up inside the cabin and a rifleman prowling outside. Maybe we should have gone after him first, but chasing a man through the woods was no easy task, and it would have given the other two a chance to make a break for their horses.

No matter. It was too late to change plans now!

In another second we no longer had the rifleman to worry about as it turned out.

I eased around the corner of the cabin and came eye to eye with Scarface holding his Winchester. Now a long gun can do a great many things that a pistol can't, but it isn't so quick at close range. He tried to shoulder the rifle but my Colt spoke first. I tagged Scarface high on the left side of his chest. The twisting .44 slug must have stopped his heart instantly. He let out a strange rattling grunt as the wind rushed from his lungs, and then just dropped over backwards, arms outflung. I stepped past the body and went toward the front of the cabin.

I remained behind the front corner of the shack for a long while, telling myself I was giving Randall time to get ready, but I knew deep down that it wasn't that which was holding me back. There were two outlaws inside the cabin with loaded, cocked weapons.

I don't know if these things come easier with experience or not, but me, I hadn't any real idea what I was going to do next.

The outlaws' tied horses were standing at the hitchrail looking at me, the whites of their eyes showing. They liked none of this. Far beyond them I could see Domino unconcernedly cropping grass beneath a cottonwood tree.

Well, I had asked for this chance. I had waited for it for a long time, now here it was. I breathed in deeply and made my move.

I took off my hat and sailed it past the window. The men inside the cabin were jittery and they fired at the first moving object they saw. I dove for the tethered horses and rolled under them. Coming up behind a big bay which sidestepped nervously at my sudden appearance, I caught a glimpse of sunlight on a gun barrel behind the half-torn oiled paper of the window and I cut loose.

I banged four shots into the window. One flew wild, tearing splinters from the frame, the others went through into the cabin. And at least one of them caught flesh.

I heard a scream like a woman's scream, saw a hand reach out and clutch at the oiled paper. Then the paper was torn away as the hand gripping it disappeared. I was pretty sure that the outlaw was dead.

Now what? Had Randall managed to dive in through the other window during the flurry of shots?

Even as the thought passed through my mind, my answer came. From inside the cabin I heard someone yell out in panic. Then shots were exchanged, perhaps six in all.

I dashed toward the front door, keeping my head down. Crossing the porch in one long stride, I slammed my shoulder into the flimsy plank door.

I saw three things at once in the dark interior of the cabin. Randall, stretched out on the floor, his head bloody, his Colt lying on the floor inches from his fingers. To my right there was a dead man. It was Brad.

And in front of me, hair in his eyes, gun leveled at me, Mike Twilly.

He fired first, but I had rolled before he squeezed the trigger. I came up as he fired again, his bullet tearing into the floorboards. From one knee I fired back and my bullet took him low in the belly.

Twilly staggered back, started to shoot again, and then just dropped his pistol. As I rose he placed a hand on his belly and pulled it away, looking in astonishment at the blood that smeared it.

"You were . . ." he began. Then he backed against the wall, still holding his belly, and sagged to a sitting position, like a doll propped up.

I walked slowly toward him, gun barrel still leveled.

"It wasn't me that wanted to kill your daddy," he wheezed as I stood over him. "Bouchonnet had some kind of grudge against him from a long way back. Don't know what it was."

"Where is Bouchonnet?" I nearly shouted. My hands and legs were shaking. So was the finger on the trigger, and Twilly saw it. He continued to talk, but not to answer my question.

"I guess . . . when your daddy was marshal . . . arrested him once for horse-stealin'," Twilly babbled on. I crouched and looked into the outlaw's eyes. They were glazing over; he didn't have long to live and we both knew it.

"Where is Bouchonnet?" I screamed. I took him by the shoulders, shaking him roughly.

He didn't answer.

He couldn't.

Holstering my revolver, I turned my attention to Randall. I had first believed him to be dead. I hadn't seen him move or heard him utter a sound. The floor around his head was stained darkly with blood, but as I rolled him over his eyes blinked open. He stared at me uncomprehendingly for a long minute and then his eyes focused and he grinned at me.

I examined his head as best I could. A bullet had cut a long furrow in his scalp from above his eye down to his ear. A flap of skin hung free, I began tearing a bandage from the tail of my shirt. I was relieved enough that I actually laughed. The bullet had stunned him as if he had been banged on the temple with a two-by-four, but he would be all right.

Randall grabbed my hand as I tried to tie the crude bandage around his head.

"Ben? Did we win?"

"It looks that way, Randall."

"Good," he said with a sigh, and he closed his eyes. "Because at first I thought . . ."

And then he passed out again.

I took Randall outside, carrying him as gently as possible. I considered burying the dead outlaws. I thought of taking them back to town.

In the end I dragged Scarface into the cabin with the others. Then I smashed a kerosene lantern on the floor. I struck a match then and set the cabin ablaze.

I pulled back into the trees where I had left Randall in the shade of a cottonwood and watched as the place burned to the ground, the roof turning black and then to gray ash which caved in and covered the outlaws' bodies.

When there was no fire left to spread, only black smoke rising to smudge the blue sky, I rounded up Domino and Randall's big black horse, the one he had "borrowed" in Natchez, and put him across the saddle for the slow ride back to La Paloma.

Chapter Thirteen

La Paloma was quiet, with only the sound of the piano from the saloon across the street drifting up to my room where I sat with Susan Gregory, both the balcony door and the hall door open for propriety and to allow the evening breeze to ventilate. There was a somber, almost sullen mood in La Paloma these days, it seemed to me.

I was finding it especially oppressive. I never had really liked this town—or any other that I could remember. Now I was wishing to shake its dust from my boots. It didn't hold a single good memory for me.

That had been settled for me when Susan came knocking and after some casual conversation she asked me to go along with her, taking the stagecoach north to Kansas where she planned to wait for Hollis Gregory, who was pushing his trail herd up that long road. I was more than willing. I was perfectly willing to go anywhere she asked me.

It was the third night following the stagecoach robbery, and the county sheriff and a deputy had arrived to hold the town down until a new marshal could be appointed. The local paper, a one-sheet, had printed the story of the big shootout Randall and I had had with the bandits, much colored, and for a time the two of us were minor heroes. That bothered me as well. Some people had shot at us, we shot back. I think Randall enjoyed it a little more than I did, but it had been three days ago and we were old news now.

"You have every reason to be happy," Susan said and I frowned at her. "You look so sad, Ben. I can't imagine why. And you don't seem to want to tell me."

"I'm sorry," I said. "I didn't realize how quiet I was being. You were saying?"

"I said you've every reason to be happy. Colin's on the mend. So's Randall. You accomplished what you came to Texas to do."

"And more," I said with a smile, watching Susan's amused eyes. Still, I sat fiddling with the object on my lap. Still my thoughts were distant.

"You've got to talk to someone, Ben, get it off your chest." Susan rose and came toward me and briefly she knelt beside me, holding my hand.

"I've told you about it."

"It's not the same, and you know it."

"I can't bring myself to do it, Susan, I just can't."

"Ben!" She rose and a bit of anger flashed in her eyes. "You must! We're leaving tomorrow and there may never be another chance."

Still I didn't respond. She breathed out sharply through her nose, a small sign of her disappointment in me. It was then that Colin McCormick appeared in the doorway, dressed in a shiny deep green suit, ruffled shirt and string tie. He was neatly barbered, using one crutch to assist him.

"I'll be back," she said in a warning tone, and she bent and kissed my forehead lightly. Nodding to McCormick, she picked up her skirts and swept from the room. Carefully, McCormick closed the door behind him as he entered.

He was studying my eyes. I had seen him watching Susan's expression. He was hardly an unobservant man. He hobbled nearer to where I sat in my wooden chair and said, "You know then."

"I know, Colin. Now."

It had taken me a while to figure it out. I should have known, but it had been so many years. I had found my Pa's watch on Twilly's body, the one they had stolen from him. The watch with the picture of my mother inside.

The picture of Cora Brighton.

The woman in the picture was much younger, of course. I had seen it before, but not frequently. There had been something vaguely familiar about Cora all along, something strange in her attitude toward me, but I hadn't figured it out immediately. Cora's hair was red for one thing. My mother, as I remembered her, had chestnut hair.

And my mother was supposed to be dead and buried in Indiana.

"Why, Colin?" I asked, lifting my eyes to the gambler.

"I suppose, Ben that—"

"I'll tell him," Cora said. She stood at the balcony door, her jaw set, her face a trifle pale. She wore lavender. A string of pearls adorned her neck. She entered the room with soundless steps. I snapped my father's watch shut, and watched Cora as she seated herself in the facing chair where Susan had been talking to me.

"I'll right," I said heavily, "tell me."

"It's not so simple, Ben . . ." She waved a hand in frustration.

"Cora is a city woman, Ben," McCormick put in, "and—"

"I said that I would tell him," Cora said a little sharply. Then to me, she said, "What Colin says is true, Ben. I am a city woman. I couldn't live on that farm for another day. Washing all of your clothes by hand, the roof leaking every time it rained, the loneliness, the isolation . . ."

"And my father couldn't take the town life?"

"No." Cora shook her head—with a touch of sadness, it seemed to me. "He did not like towns. Nor people. Nor guns! Especially not guns. He came home one night here, in La Paloma, and told me that he was through with the old life. He had only enemies in this town, in Texas. He wanted a peaceful place to live out his years without wondering if the next man he passed wanted to shoot him in the back. He threw his gunbelt to the floor and swore he would never fire a gun in anger again. He would buy a small farm far away from everyone.

"It all sounded fine—to him. For me it meant leaving all my friends, having no church even! Nowhere to go of an evening, no restaurant, no newspaper. Only hogs and chickens and the loneliness . . . the loneliness."

"And so you just upped and left. Left me as well," I said bitterly.

"I just left, yes."

"You see, Ben—" McCormick tried to interject, but this time I cut him off angrily.

"And just where do you come into this, Colin? What are you to my mother exactly?"

He glanced at Cora. "Friends, Ben. Believe me, we are just good friends." He paused. "I wanted it to be more, but . . ."

"But I was still married to your father, Ben," Cora said. "I would do nothing like that."

I shook my head. I was trying to be fair, but maybe I wasn't. I hadn't walked in her shoes.

I could imagine a girl from town trying that mud and bramble farm life, her hands growing rough, her hair starting to gray. No neighbors. The loneliness . . .

maybe I did understand. Maybe I should have tried harder to understand both of my parents.

Really, I hadn't known my father either. I hadn't even known he had once been a town marshal. I hadn't known that he had quit and bought that Kentucky farm, or why. But I *did* know how my father had felt about killing men. That had been imbued in me. The killing I had done still weighed heavily on my own conscience; I hoped to never be forced to kill again.

Maybe I needed now to try harder to understand. Perhaps it was time to banish the hurt boy inside and be man enough to forgive.

"I still don't understand where you fit in, Colin."

Cora answered. "Don't you, Ben? Really? Your father couldn't make a living on that farm. He tried, but he was no farmer. He was a lawman! I knew that he wasn't doing well and you didn't have much, but—"

"But most of what you did have came from your mother," McCormick put in firmly. "I know because that was my job. To take a few dollars up there now and again and see that you at least had shoes and a winter coat."

Cora interrupted. She stretched open hands toward me in a pleading gesture. "But mainly I needed to know how you were doing, Ben. How you had grown. What you looked like, what kind of man you were growing into. I couldn't go back myself, obviously, and so I used to send Colin to Gorse from time to time just to check on you, so he could come and tell me . . . how you were getting on." Her voice broke a little and a single tear, quickly wiped away, started down her cheek.

To McCormick I said, "So that's why you took me in so quickly on the riverboat, let me into your cabin. Gave me money." All of those pieces of the puzzle became suddenly clear.

He didn't answer. Cora still watched me intently. Her eyes were damp, her mouth compressed as if she wanted to speak but would not allow herself to say what she wished to say.

With a great effort she let the words flow free. "I know your feelings were hurt, Ben. Since your boyhood you've carried doubts and unhappy longings, but—"

"But now its time to get past all of that!" Susan said in a remarkably cheerful voice. She had come back into the room without anyone having been aware of it, so intent were we all on the conversation. "Isn't it, Ben?"

I was thinking of many things. I remembered the look on Cora's face the day of the stage robbery as she forced her way through the mob. *Who is it? Who's hurt?* Her expression had been frantic.

It was me she had been worried about, not McCormick.

I felt ashamed of my petulance, my childish words. I did not know what to do now. I felt exceedingly awkward. I rose to my feet but remained fixed where I was until Susan stepped beside me and took my elbow, guiding me forward.

Then my arms were around Cora. My mother. And

she was crying. I'd say I was crying too, but I don't want to admit it. Maybe my eyes were a little misty, nothing more. Cora just kept stroking my head, petting me and I suddenly realized how lucky I was! Just as Susan had tried to convince me.

After all, I thought I had lost my mother forever. Thought she had died and I would never see her again. And here she was! Right in my arms.

"I feel so damned stupid!" I managed to say, but no one replied. After a long minute I stepped back. Cora and I held hands at arms' length and just looked at each other for a long while before our fingers slipped away.

"Well, now," McCormick said in a husky voice that betrayed his own emotions. "What about the future, Ben? You know you're pretty popular around La Paloma right now. You've shown that you have the right stuff for the job. If you wanted to consider taking the job of town marshal . . ."

"I've got a better offer," I said quickly.

"A better . . . ?" My mother was confused.

"We're leaving on the stage for Kansas tomorrow," Susan told them. "Ben and me."

"Kansas! What's in Kansas for you?"

"My father, of course!" Susan said. "After all, we should ask his permission, shouldn't we?"

Stunned, Cora looked at McCormick, then at me, and finally to Susan. She stretched out her arms and took Susan to her breast, hugging her tightly.

"Congratulations," Colin said, taking my hand.

"We'll be coming back," Susan said. "If Ben wants to."

"I do." The Grapevine was a fine ranch. I could live out my years there happily. With Susan.

I had a suggestion. "I know another local hero who has made up his mind that he no longer wishes to be a cowboy, but he just might make a fine town marshal."

"You don't mean that redheaded critter sitting downstairs in the lobby with his head all wrapped up in bandages?" McCormick asked.

I laughed. "Yes, I do. Ask Randall. He's decided he doesn't care as much as he once thought for watching the rear ends of steers. The marshal's job might just prove more to his liking."

Morning dawned bright and clear, though off to the north some heavy thunderheads were beginning to build. After hugs and best wishes all around, Susan and I clambered aboard the stage for Abilene. It would be a three-day trip, but we would reach Kansas long before the slow-moving trail herd.

We leaned out to wave good-bye to McCormick, his arm around my mother who was crying just a little, and to Randall, who grinned that toothless grin of his. He lifted his hat off his bandaged head, and waved it in the air.

Then we were gone, rocking and swaying, rolling across the long flat land, Susan sitting close beside me.

It rained the first night out and we spent the night in a leaky, log way station, but after that we had good weather. Our spirits were high, anyway. We didn't care if it was rain or shine. I don't think a broken axle or Kiowas could have affected our joyful mood.

Still, it was a relief to finally climb down off the stage at Abilene. The town was blessedly quiet, not living up to its reputation for the moment. There were no rambunctious cowboys tearing the town apart. The people who lived there were actually looking forward to the arrival of the first big trail herd of the year—Hollis Gregory's steers. The cattlemen, after all, were the reason for the town's existence and its chief source of income.

There was little for me to do in Abilene as we waited. I accompanied Susan on a dozen shopping trips, waiting patiently while she discussed this dress or that, shoes and ribbons and buttons and bolts of material. I didn't begrudge her the spree. It would be a long time before she was again able to shop in a fair-sized town like Abilene.

We ate at the better restaurants and had rooms in a nice hotel. I wandered around by the railroad tracks sometimes, watching the trains come and go. They were still new in the West and fascinating with their power. One night I played cards with a few men in the hotel cardroom, and lost of course. That was about it. I was beginning to get antsy, wanting to get back to Texas, wanting to take Susan as my bride.

It was the fourth morning there as I was walking

from the stable where I'd gone to eyeball a horse for the buggy that Susan and I planned to use to travel back home with, when I turned the corner into an alley and walked right into Bouchonnet.

Chapter Fourteen

There was a long moment when time seemed to freeze as I found myself face to face with the redheaded man with the cruel mouth and killing eyes. The man who had murdered my father. Bouchonnet had his pistol drawn, yet he, too, stood immobile for a time, glaring at me, perhaps savoring victory.

"You should have gotten off my trail," he growled finally. "You should never have come to Kansas."

"You were the last thing on my mind when—" I saw Bouchonnet's thumb caress the hammer of his Colt and I threw myself to one side, landing roughly behind a pile of barrels as his shot rang out, echoing down the dusty alleyway.

I managed to draw and fire in return, but I was shooting from my back and the shot went very high and wide. A second bullet from Bouchonnet's gun punched through an oaken barrel, narrowly missing my head, close enough so that a long jagged splinter imbedded itself in my cheek.

"Here, here! Knock it off. I'm sending for the marshal!" we heard someone yelling from the head of the alley. I saw Bouchonnet spin around and fire at the unsuspecting intruder, driving him to cover.

In that instant I leaped up and rushed across the scant distance between myself and Bouchonnet. I launched my shoulder at Bouchonnet's knees and drove him into the ground, his head thumping back roughly against the alley floor. The pistol flew from his hands.

Bouchonnet was stronger than he looked. He slammed a fist against my skull and I had to blink away the stars.

He tried to struggle to his feet, me clinging to one of his boots. The other boot he swung at my head, falling again as he did so. The boot grazed my temple.

When Bouchonnet fought free again, I had lost my grip on his foot. I saw him dive for his pistol, but I was still quick enough to scuttle that way on hands and knees and beat him to it. With both of my hands on the Colt, he couldn't take it from me. He contented himself with kicking me once more, in the ribs this time, and the breath rushed out of my lungs in pain.

I was still on hands and knees, his pistol under my hand, but I could not manage to get a grip on it and I was losing the fight. Several more men had appeared at the head of the alley in response to the shots, and Bouchonnet, seeing them, took to his heels and raced away.

Now I was on my feet, holding my side and I staggered after him in a loping, awkward run. The men behind me yelled scrambled questions. I didn't try to answer. I just ran on.

I had Bouchonnet in sight as we reached a crossing alley, but he was far ahead of me and running much faster. I was younger and raised in the Kentucky woods, where running was a pleasure and joy, but with my head ringing and my ribs shot through with pain, with my lungs starved for air, I couldn't make up any ground on the killer.

We had reached the outskirts of town and Bouchonnet still ran on. Now and then he would look across his shoulder to determine if I was following. I was, nothing could have stopped me. Nothing but a killing, and Bouchonnet was without a gun.

We reached the train tracks, where cottonwood trees and sumac crowded against the silver rails. Bouchonnet, running weakly now so that he resembled a marionette as he wobbled on his way, crossed the rails, stumbling over a tie. He managed to stay on his feet, however, and by the time I reached the tracks, he had vanished into the trees and brush beyond.

I stopped for one deep, painful breath and ran on.

I wove through the tangle of undergrowth, paying no heed to the branches and thorns that cut at my body. I was aware of only one emotion, the emotion of a hunting animal in pursuit of its quarry.

Bursting out of the brush, I could see the Abilene stockyards ahead. Cattle milled and lowed, waiting to be shipped north. No one was around that I could see.

Nor could I see Bouchonnet.

I stood there, gasping for air, fearing that I had lost him back among the trees and brush. Then I sighted him again, running in a crouch, his face twisted with fear and with anger. He looked at me, cursed, and climbed between the rails of the cattle pen and lost himself among the hundreds of cattle.

I followed him, feeling stronger with each stride now as my breathing eased. The throbbing in my skull I simply ignored.

I ducked under a rail myself and began pushing my way through the cattle. The heat generated by their close-packed bodies was tremendous. There was only the stink and the heat of the cattle, their long horns occasionally clacking together in those close quarters. I could see nothing of Bouchonnet.

Risking being trampled, I went to the foul ground and peered under the cattle, looking through the forest of their legs.

And I spotted him.

I saw his boots and trousers not fifteen feet from me and I shoved aside a brindle steer, heedless of the danger, and went after Bouchonnet.

He rose up suddenly, but not where I expected him to

be. He dove over the back of a black steer, the knife in his hand flashing silver in the Kansas sun and we went to the ground together. I felt the pistol in my hand fall free of my grip. Bouchonnet was on top of me and he slashed down with his knife. I rolled my head away from the blade, drove my knee up into his groin and he grunted with pain. The hoofs of the disturbed cattle were all around us. I narrowly avoided having my head stepped on and ground into the muck of the pen.

I tried to scramble to my feet, but Bouchonnet grabbed my belt and pulled me back. His other hand snaked out, the edge of the knife blade grazing my side just above the belt line. I could feel hot blood rushing from the wound.

Fear and anger made me into a wildman. I twisted and shoved and punched out with both hands, kicking savagely.

One of my blows caught Bouchonnet enough so that he staggered back, his eye filming over. He backed away from me and was brought up abruptly as he backed into a huge speckled longhorn.

Enraged, the steer turned its head and hooked Bouchonnet with its horn. I could only gawk in horror.

The big longhorn had a spread of six feet or so—dangerous, needle-pointed horns—and as Bouchonnet screamed loudly, I saw its horn penetrate his back just above the kidney and poke out through his belly.

The longhorn tossed its head and the gored Bouchonnet was tossed off like a child's doll. When he landed he was awash in his own blood, his blue shirt stained purple. His face was caked with manure and dust. The cattle had bawled and shoved each other away from the disturbance. I went to where the killer lay and knelt down.

"I'll get you a doctor," I said.

"Go to hell," he panted. "I'm a goner. Why did you have to follow me here, Jury?"

"I wasn't looking for you, Bouchonnet. I only wished to be finished with the killing. You could have just gone on your way free."

"But you . . . !" Then he began to laugh, to laugh outrageously until blood flowed from his mouth, strangling off the laugh and his life.

His eyes were open wide, staring at the hot Kansas sky. I think he was trying to say something else at the end, but I'll never know what it was.

I rose shakily and dusted off as best I could. My own side was still bleeding, my head still ached and I was sick to my stomach from what I had seen. I started back through the herd, moving very carefully so as not to set them off, until I reached the rails of the pen.

I crawled through them and then just collapsed. I saw a group of three men running toward me like men emerging from a mirage. I was grateful to them, for I could not make it any farther on my own. I closed my eyes and passed gently into a dark and soothing void.

Chapter Fifteen

Susan and I had begun building our own house on Grapevine. After the wedding Hollis Gregory had appointed me ranch manager. I still had a lot to learn about the cattle business, but I was working hard at it.

Doyle remained foreman. He and I had made up. I don't know if that was because of my new status or because he had finally managed to put the old feud out of his mind, but we got along well enough to work together, and that was all that mattered.

Choctaw Kilbride had reappeared from his expedition and we took him on as yard hand, a job he seemed to like despite a lifetime spent as a wandering man.

Despite his youth Randall Hawse was appointed town marshal. I helped him take care of some paper-

214

work now and then, and with the business of restitution. That is, for the black horse he had stolen in Natchez.

We ran an advertisement in the Natchez newspapers saying, *The marshal of La Paloma, Texas, has recovered a horse believed to have been stolen in Natchez. The horse is a tall black which owner may claim by writing and further identifying the animal.* Which was an easy matter for the true owner. The black had two brands on one hip, another on the right front shoulder, and one of his ears was notched, presumably bitten by another horse.

Or, our advertisement went on, *the owner may request reasonable payment for said animal if he does not wish to travel to La Paloma to claim it.*

Eventually a man name Claghorne did identify the horse in a letter. He didn't have any interest in riding all the way to Texas to recover the black and he and Randall agreed on a fair price. Randall rode that horse for the next ten years, and in that time became a well-respected, canny lawman.

Randall also wrote an explanatory note to the Natchez marshal to take me off the wanted list—which was accepted, much to my relief.

It was not more than three weeks after Susan and I got back from Kansas that we received a notice that was no real surprise to us. McCormick and my mother—Cora Brighton—were to be married in the town church. The wedding was held on a cool, sunny day, and everything went well except there was a lot of crying and carrying on by the womenfolk.

There's little more to say. Life is pleasant and easy on Grapevine. Everyone is well, and the Brazos runs on silver-bright and untamed as it will till the end of time.